"I DON'T THINK MAYBE
HE TAKE MUCH MORE, KEINO."

The boy's face was badly swollen. His nose, crooked and smashed to one side, was obviously broken. His right eye had received so many blows that white, glimmering bone now showed where an eyebrow should have been.

The big man raised an arm and wiped the small rivers of sweat from his face. "I no think he will live if I beat more on him," he said. "He die—then we no find out nothing you want to know."

Keino slid off the barstool. Crossing the room, he stopped beside the chair. "You are correct, my friend. So be it." Before Sebota could move out of the way, Keino pulled a pistol from behind his back and shot the boy through the head. Blood and parts of brain splattered across Sebota's chest. The big man's first instinct was to yell out at the killer, but the depraved look in Keino's eyes quickly diminished the thought.

Julius Keino had been out of prison less than twenty-four hours, and already the killing had begun.

Other Avon Books by
James N. Pruitt

LOBO ONE

FIRE FORCE

JAMES N. PRUITT

AVON BOOKS ✦ NEW YORK

FIRE FORCE is an original publication of Avon Books. This work has never before appeared in book form. This work is a novel. Any similarity to actual persons or events is purely coincidental.

AVON BOOKS
A division of
The Hearst Corporation
1350 Avenue of the Americas
New York, New York 10019

Copyright © 1992 by James Pruitt
Published by arrangement with the author
Library of Congress Catalog Card Number: 91-92452
ISBN: 0-380-76617-5

First Avon Books Printing: May 1992

AVON TRADEMARK REG. U.S. PAT. OFF. AND IN OTHER COUNTRIES, MARCA REGISTRADA, HECHO EN U.S.A.

Printed in the U.S.A.

RA   10   9   8   7   6   5   4   3   2   1

CHAPTER ONE

Rutherford Hayes retrieved his overnight bag from the carousel luggage rack and walked to the exit doors of Los Angeles International Airport. A skycap asked him if he needed a taxi. Hayes shook his head no as he placed the overnight bag near the curb. He retained a fine leather briefcase, holding it securely in his left hand. Glancing at his watch, the husky, sixty-year-old man with salt-and-pepper hair made a mental note, upon his return to Langley, Virginia, to send a memo to the L.A. office regarding punctuality. Rutherford Hayes had few obsessions in his life, but adherence to schedule was definitely one that topped his list.

The minutes passed. Reaching into the side pocket of his suit coat, he felt around for his cigarettes. Then he remembered that he had quit smoking a week before at the insistence of his loving but nagging wife and the lectures he was constantly subjected to by the surgeon general every time they met at the White House. He was just about to take the skycap's earlier offer when he saw a black limousine swing onto the up ramp that led to the terminal. Hayes recognized the special government license plate on the front bumper.

"About time," muttered Hayes to himself as he bent down and picked up his bag. "Sad day when the director of the CIA can't get a ride in L.A."

The car pulled to the curb and stopped directly in front of Hayes. A young man in his early twenties leaped from the car and rushed around to open the trunk. He took the director's bag and opened the side door, as he said, "Sorry for the delay, sir, but the Los Angeles traffic is murder this time of day."

Hayes frowned but did not say anything as he stepped into the luxury automobile. The young man placed the bag in the trunk, closed it, then slid in behind the wheel. Not wanting to make two mistakes in the same day, the driver looked back over his shoulder and asked, "Sir, do you want to stop by our main office before going to WISCO?"

Hayes, his irritability eased slightly now that he had settled into the comfort of the limousine, replied, "No, let's go on to WISCO. Mr. Richards is expecting me. I don't want to keep him waiting."

The driver nodded as he said, "The information you requested, sir, is on disk and has already been loaded into the computer."

"Thank you," answered Hayes as the limousine pulled away from the curb and headed for downtown Los Angeles.

Hayes pressed a button located on the center arm-rest next to his right hand. A sliding panel opened in the divider behind the driver's seat. Reaching forward, Hayes tapped a key marked 'access'. The computer screen came to life. The words, WISCO—World International Security Corporation, appeared in gold letters on a blue background. Removing the special remote control designed for the computer, Hayes sat back in his seat and pressed the 'enter' button on the control. The screen went blank for a moment, then showed a detailed biography of the WISCO organization.

World International Security Corp.
Chief Executive Officer: Erin W. Richards—Colonel (Retired) Twenty-three years active duty U.S. Army (Airborne, Ranger, Special Forces qualified) Age: 58.

Four combat tours—Republic of Vietnam. Highly decorated: Distinguished Service Cross (2 Awards), Silver Star (3 Awards), Bronze Star for Valor (4 Awards), Purple Heart (6 Awards).

Former Instructor—U.S. Army War College, 4 years.

Honor Graduate, British Special Air Services Commando School, England.

Last Assignment: Commander—U.S. Anti-terrorist unit Delta Force, Fort Bragg, North Carolina.

Retired active service May, 1985.

Established WISCO January, 1986. Corporate headquarters located at 2503 Wilshire Blvd, Los Angeles, California.

WISCO Concept: Provide high intensity, low profile security on an international scale to industrial, commercial, and private corporations with emphasis placed on personal protection of key individuals. In five years, WISCO has become a highly respected organization with an excellent reputation for success. Minimum fee for WISCO services which involve extensive operations is one million dollars.

Personnel Status: WISCO maintains a headquarters staff of over 100 under the direction of Vice President and Assistant CEO, Randy York, retired Special Forces Major and former executive officer of the Delta Force under Colonel Richards. Mr. York provided fifty percent of the capital to begin WISCO and is a full partner in the organization. It is estimated that WISCO presently has a total of 250 field operatives worldwide.

All operatives are former military personnel with prominent background skills in unconventional warfare and special operations. These skills include, but are not limited to, light and heavy weapons, demolitions, tactics, communications, medicine and terrorists—anti-terrorists operations. Extensive background investigation and personal approval by Colonel Richards and Major York is required for employment with the WISCO organization. Ninety-five percent of all contracts accepted by this organization are considered to be high risk operations. Field operatives are compensated accordingly, with the minimum salary set at $5,000 per month.

In the five years since its inception, WISCO has sustained a known total of fifty-two operatives killed and eighty-six wounded; twenty-one of this number resulting in permanent disability. However, all employees are fully insured by the corporation in the amount of $100,000 each, which is paid promptly to the beneficiary in the event of the employee's death. Those wounded who receive a disabling injury are granted full retirement benefits of $3,500 per month, plus full compensation of all medical expenses for life.

Present dollar value of WISCO and total assets is one hundred twenty-one million dollars.

This information current as of March, 1991.

. . . . END OF FILE . . . .

"Damn," muttered Hayes to himself as he reached forward and turned off the computer, "with benefits like that, I wouldn't mind working for WISCO myself."

"You say something, sir?" asked the driver, glancing up into his rearview mirror.

"No, nothing, son. I was just talking to myself. That's all," said Hayes, closing the panel on the computer. Sitting back in the plush comfort of the seat, he stared out the window at the L.A. Music Center and the Civic Center as they came up on the right. It had been quite some time since he had last been in Los Angeles, but little had changed. The smog was as thick as ever, and everyone still drove thirty miles an hour over the speed limit. He who hesitated on a California freeway was lost; it was not an atmosphere for the faint of heart. As they approached Wilshire, the traffic was bumper to bumper and moving at a snail's pace. Rutherford Hayes decided to forget the memo to the Los Angeles office regarding punctuality.

The limo edged over into the turn lane, then swung out of the crowded traffic and disappeared into the tunnel leading to an underground parking area designated for WISCO. The car slowed, crossed over two rather excessively large speed bumps, and proceeded downward. Hayes sat up alertly, staring out the tinted windows, surprised that they had been permitted to advance the fifty yard length of the well lighted tunnel without being challenged.

The building was a steel and glass structure that reached ten stories into the L.A. sky. Rutherford Hayes felt a chill shoot down his spine as his mind flashed back to another time and another place: the time, 23 October, 1983, 0615—it was a Sunday morning; the place, the headquarters of the Marine Battalion Landing Team near the airport at Beirut, Lebanon. A seemingly innocent looking yellow Mercedes truck, a racing engine, and an inexperienced young sentry at the gate, proved to be a deadly combination. Within seconds, the truck loaded with explosives was past the guard before he could lock a round into the chamber of his weapon and fire. Those were precious seconds lost that ultimately cost the lives of 241 U.S. Marines and wounded more than a hundred others. It was one of the most devastating acts of terrorism Hayes had ever seen in his lifetime. Memories of that day would remain with him forever: the twisted, shattered bodies of Marines lying in piles on the ground, their arms and legs dangling grotesquely. He could still hear the screams and moans of the injured and the dying as they lay trapped beneath a smoldering heap of thirty-foot-high rubble of shattered stone that had once been a four-story, concrete building. It was only after this sad sacrifice that the government of the United States realized the seriousness of the terrorist problem and the power of these killers to achieve political and military objectives through such terrorism. This single act had achieved exactly what was intended, the withdrawal of American forces from Lebanon. It was a hell of a thought to be having while traveling through a tunnel beneath a ten-story building; but, nevertheless, a nightmare that refused to go away. Hayes doubted it ever would. From what he had seen so far, WISCO was a prime candidate for just such an attack.

Finding a slot marked 'Visitors', the driver parked the car. Stepping out, he opened the door for the director and pointed to a large concrete and glass booth near an elevator surrounded by a dull red light.

"You'll have to show your identification to the guards in that booth before you go up, sir. Mr. Richards' office is on the tenth floor."

Hayes nodded his thanks. Taking the briefcase with him, he walked the short distance to the booth. The two men inside were in their early thirties, dressed in black slacks, light blue shirts with red epaulets, and black ties. They watched him closely as he approached. As they stood up from behind their consoles, Hayes saw the dull black pistol grips of the 9mm Berettas protruding from the shoulder holsters worn by each man. From the looks of the two, it was apparent they knew how to use the weapons if they had to.

Stepping in front of the glass, Hayes said, "Rutherford Hayes, I have an appointment with Mr. Richards."

While one of the guards called upstairs, the other stared down at the briefcase and asked, "Would you please place your briefcase on the table to your left, sir, and step back?"

Hayes did as he was instructed.

"Thank you," said the security man, politely, as he reached down and fingered the multi-switched console. He studied the images of the briefcase's contents on the series of monitors that lined the small room in front of him.

Hayes watched with experienced interest as the x-rayed contents of his case flashed onto the screens. Judging from the thickness of the glass, he assumed that the security unit's booth was bullet-proof. The man on the phone replaced the receiver and moved to the glass in front of Hayes. Pressing a microphone switch inside the blockhouse, he asked, "Could I see your identification, sir?"

Hayes reached into the side pocket of his charcoal gray suit, removed his wallet and held out his government identification card. The guard hit another switch and a small stainless steel tray slid out from the base of the glass. "Place it in the tray, please," requested the guard.

The director smiled to himself as he placed the card on the tray. It disappeared back into the booth. Looking up, Hayes noticed three surveillance cameras located atop the booth. They covered every possible angle of approach to the elevator. This was the type of security he expected of an organization with WISCO's reputation.

The guard with his identification card stepped to a computer, tapped in some information; then returned the card to the tray. Pressing the switch again, the tray slid back out, and Hayes recovered the card. As he picked it up, the security man said, "Mr. Hayes, sir, would you please place your left thumb on the red plastic disk located on the left side of the tray please?"

WISCO was now exceeding Hayes' expectations. Placing his thumb where requested, he watched in surprise as the fingerprint of his left thumb was transferred to a computer color monitor. His thumb print was compared to a second print on another computer. Multi-colored lines traced each ridge of the heat transferred print for precise detail. Both computers echoed a soft 'beep', and the word "Cleared" appeared on both computer screens. The guard smiled politely as he said, "Thank you, Mr. Hayes. If you will take your case and step in front of the elevator, I will open the doors for you. Mr. Richards is expecting you. Mr. York will meet you on the tenth floor when you exit the elevator. Thank you for your cooperation, and have a nice day, sir."

Stepping to the elevator doors, Hayes stood quietly, staring blankly at the steel doors. He was still trying to figure out how, and where, Richards and WISCO had come up with the fingerprints of the director of the Central Intelligence Agency.

There was a sound of an electronic bolt being released as the elevator doors opened silently. Hayes looked along the sides of the elevator for a button to push that would take him to the tenth floor. There was no control panel inside. Bewildered, he stared out at the security booth. The security men inside waved as the doors closed. He heard the bolt lock back into place. The elevator occupants could not exit until the elevator reached the specific level programmed by the computer. "I'm impressed," whispered Hayes. "These boys put on quite a show."

The elevator began its ascent toward the top floor. Hayes was still pondering the question of the fingerprint when soft music began to play from the overhead speakers in the elevator. "I'll be damned," said Hayes. The tune was an ear-pleasing rendition of, 'Danny Boy,' performed by the London Philharmonic. It was Rutherford Hayes' favorite piece of music.

The elevator came to a stop so smoothly that Hayes did not realize that he had already reached his destination. The doors opened. There in front of him stood a big man in his early forties. It was Randy York, vice-president of WISCO. York was a handsome man. He stood six-foot-four, with wide shoulders, dark hair, and blue-green eyes that reflected a pleasant welcome. Reaching out a bear-like hand, York grasped the director's as he said, "Mr. Hayes, I'm Randy York. Welcome to World International Security. Mr. Richards is waiting in his office."

"The pleasure is mine, sir," replied Hayes, admiring the fine cut of the dark blue suit worn by the big man as they shook hands. It would cost Hayes two months' pay for a suit like that.

York released the man's hand and motioned down the hall. "If you will follow me, sir, I'll take you to Mr. Richards."

Hayes nodded and fell in alongside York as they walked to the end of the hall and entered an outer office. An attractive young woman with flowing blonde hair glanced up from her typewriter as the two men entered. "Suzie, this is Mr. Hayes. Mr. Richards is expecting us. Please hold all our calls. I'm not certain how long this will take."

The blue-eyed beauty flashed a smile showing perfect, glistening white teeth as she directed her charming gaze to York. "Of course, Mr. York. Would you gentlemen like coffee?"

"Maybe a little later. I'll let you know," said York, as he tapped on the door before entering Erin Richards' office.

The president of WISCO was standing at the huge smoked glass panels that formed the wall behind his desk and staring out across the vastness of Los Angeles. He turned as the two men entered the room.

"Ah, Mr. Hayes. How are you, sir?" asked Richards, coming from behind his desk and crossing the center of the room with his hand outstretched. "It is an honor to have you visit, sir. Quite an honor indeed."

Hayes shook hands as he quickly sized up Erin Richards. The report on the computer in the limousine had stated that this man was fifty-eight years old, but that could not possibly be correct. This man didn't look a day over forty. His shoulders were broad and straight, his chest wide, and tapered down to a narrow waist. His grip was warm, but firm. The only visible sign of age was in his face. It held a weathered and worn look. His eyes were dark brown. Small lines weaved their way beneath them like a roadmap. Dark hair, streaked with silver, topped off this stout looking man of distinction.

"The pleasure is mine, Mr. Richards," said Hayes as they moved to the desk. York motioned for the director to take a seat on the overstuffed, black leather couch in front of the desk. "Can I get you coffee or anything before we start, sir?" asked York before sitting down. Hayes shook his head, no. He would wait until later. Richards moved around behind his desk, pulled out the high-backed chair and sat down. Clasping his hands together in front of him on the desktop, he asked, "Well, now, Mr. Hayes, just what can we at WISCO do for you?"

The CIA director placed his briefcase on his lap. Removing a folder from inside, he leaned forward and passed it across the desk to Richards. "It would seem we have a rather unusual situation on our hands, Mr. Richards. Do you recognize the man in that first photo?"

Richards opened the folder. A color 8x10 photograph was attached to the left side of the folder with a paper clip. It was a picture of a black man dressed in tiger stripe combat fatigues, a black beret, with a Russian AK-47 assault rifle slung across his chest. There was a stubble of beard around his face. Large black eyes in pools of white stared out from the rugged looking, black African face. The short remains of a cigar hung from the left side of his pale red lips. Richards studied the picture for a moment. Richards was a man of exceptional recollection. He possessed the gift of a photographic memory. He had seen this photo somewhere before. Tapping his finger against the side of his cheek, he allowed the flashes of his gifted memory to sort through volumes of pictures in his mind. Then, suddenly, there it was. With confidence, he looked up at Hayes, "General Moise Tobutu—former guerrilla leader of the Shona Nationalist faction during the Rhodesian uprisings of the seventies. This picture made the cover of *Newsweek* in June of 1976."

Hayes was impressed, and it showed in his face as Richards continued, "Tobutu was one of three popular black leaders chosen to share control with Prime Minister Ian Smith after an 'internal settlement' was signed in March 1978. A majority of the guerrilla leaders didn't care for the idea of shared control of the government; they wanted it all. Tobutu made the mistake of accepting the plan for a united election to be held in '79. Although his action won the backing of the people, the more radical leaders were afraid they couldn't win an election that would place their Communist indoctrinated leaders into power. Tobutu simply wanted to end the bloodshed and start rebuilding the country. So did a majority of the people."

Richards paused, removed a cigar from the box on his right. Between puffs, he continued.

"Tobutu was to have been one of the men on the 1979 ballot, but he never got the chance. Two weeks before the elections, 'unidentified' sources ambushed his family and him outside the town of Rhwanei—his wife and two of his children were killed. Tobutu was shot six times and left for dead, but he somehow survived. At Tobutu's request, the prime minister secretly had Tobutu and his two remaining children smuggled out of the country. The elections were a total disaster that resulted in charges and countercharges of corruption on the part of whites and blacks alike. That year over four thousand people died before a peace treaty was finally signed in December of 1980. Rhodesia became Zimbabwe and little has been heard of General Moise Tobutu since that time." Richards closed the folder, smiled across the desk at Hayes, and asked, "How did I do, Mr. Hayes?"

"Remarkable, to say the least, sir," replied Hayes. The CIA director's evaluation of Erin Richards had just increased one hundredfold. The man had done no more than look at a photo; and then, without turning a single page of the report, he had condensed the entire stack of intelligence information into a two-minute history lesson.

"Thank you, sir," answered Richards. "Apparently your reason for being here involves General Tobutu. How can we help you?"

Hayes shifted in his chair and began, "Mr. Richards, you may or may not be aware that elections are scheduled for this year in Zimbabwe."

Richards leaned back in his chair. A small puff of smoke curled its way toward the ceiling vents as he said, "Scheduled for mid-October: five candidates—three Communist-backed, one doctor with good intentions, and a province selectman entered as a ploy by the Communists to give the elections a look of legitimacy."

Hayes saw the beginnings of a grin breaking out at the corner of Randy York's lips. Hayes suddenly realized how stupid his statement about the elections had been. Here was a man who ran an international organization which provided security around the world. Of course he would know about the elections in Zimbabwe. However, knowledge of the breakdown of the candidates was a welcome surprise. It was going to make his job that much easier.

"Well, I guess that answers that question," said Hayes, with an edge of humor. "So let's dump the chitchat and get right to it. The people of Zimbabwe have had ten years of rule under the thumb of the Communist-backed radicals who claimed victory in 1980, and they've had it with them. There is a popular movement within the country to bring General Tobutu out of exile and place him at the head of the list of candidates for this year's elections. From all intelligence reports we have managed to gather throughout the country, we believe he could easily carry the popular vote and become the new leader of Zimbabwe. It would mark the first time in ten years that a man without political connections or obligations to any group or country other than his own has held that position."

Richards cast an icy stare in Hayes' direction and spoke softly as he asked, "No obligations or connections, Mr. Hayes? Our country's going to help him out just for the hell of it, right? You'll excuse me, sir, but I find that rather hard to believe. No one, especially the U.S., gives something for nothing. Those days are long gone."

Hayes shifted in his chair again, displaying only the slightest hint of nervousness as he did so. Clearing his throat, he said, "Do I detect a note of cynicism, Mr. Richards?"

"You're damn right you do, sir. Don't forget, I spent over twenty years carrying out this country's 'no obligations' policies from Vietnam to El Salvador. In short, Mr. Hayes, don't piss down my back and try to convince me it's raining, okay? Now, what exactly do you plan to gain from this 'no commitment' election?"

Hayes had not planned on going into classified details, but it was obvious that Erin Richards had a better grip on the realities of the real world than most. Any attempts to conjure up an unlikely cover story would serve no purpose. The truth, classified or not, was the only way to deal with Erin Richards.

"Very well, Mr. Richards, I will level with you. However, this information is classified, and I expect you and Mr. York will respect that fact. As you have stated, the elections are scheduled for mid-October. That is less than one month away. On October the first, the government of South Africa plans to release Julius Keino from prison."

The name brought a startled look to Richards's face. He straightened in his chair, shock in his eyes. Randy York slumped back against the couch, and a low whistle escaped his lips as he said, "I don't fucking believe it."

Richards expressed similar disbelief. "You can't be serious! Julius Keino was the black guerrilla leader who massacred over nine hundred white Rhodesian men, women, and children in the town of Gwanda in 1975. The bastard should have been hung when they captured him in South Africa. Would have been, too, if it hadn't been for all the damn bleeding-heart liberals in this country and Europe."

Hayes was glad he had decided to be honest with Richards. It was obvious that the ex-Delta Force commander would not hesitate to support any group going up against Julius Keino.

"You are absolutely correct, Mr. Richards. However, that was not the case. Now, fifteen years later, those same bleeding hearts have applied such vast economical and political pressure on the South Africans that they have little choice but to free the son-of-a-bitch. He plans to run as a candidate in the Zimbabwe elections. Our sources within the radical government report that steps are now under way to steal those elections and place Julius Keino in the presidential palace."

Erin Richards shook his head sadly, "My God, the man is a homicidal maniac. He'll make Idi Amin's reign of terror over Uganda look like a Sunday social event, and that bastard killed over two hundred thousand of his own damn people. With Keino running the country, there won't be a white person left alive after thirty days. The man screams apartheid, and he's the worst racist of the bunch. Damnit!" said Richards, raising his voice louder than intended. "Sorry, Mr. Hayes, I'm afraid I allow myself to become too emotional on occasion. Now, just what exactly do you and your people have in mind to halt this unfortunate turn turn of events?"

More relaxed now, Hayes looked at Richards and said, "Tobutu—he's the key. We believe that his popularity among the people is so strong that attempts at anything other than a fair election will cause the people to turn on the radical elements that seek to take over and place this madman in power."

"Your intelligence supports that evaluation, sir?" asked Randy York.

"Yes, Mr. York, and it is highly reliable, I might add. If Tobutu can return to Zimbabwe by next week and begin a relentless campaign throughout the country, then, we believe, he will be elected by a landslide. The present government of Zimbabwe has given in to the demands of the people and openly invited the exiled general to return for the elections. They feel that since Tobutu has been out of the country for nearly sixteen years, he poses no threat to their plan."

"What is General Tobutu's opinion of all of this?" asked Richards.

"I spoke with the general yesterday. He has agreed to return, much to the disapproval of his two remaining sons. They wanted to return with their father, but he refused. He wants them to finish college. They are both honor students at the University of Southern California. Tobutu realizes the risks. But he sees little future for his country under the present regime, and none at all if Julius Keino becomes the next president. He is willing to take those risks if there is a chance to save Zimbabwe."

Richards placed the tips of his fingers together and slowly tapped them against his chin as he looked across at Hayes. Then he said, "You realize, of course, that once Keino sees they have misjudged the general's popularity, they will kill him."

"They will try," replied Hayes in a serious tone. "That is where WISCO comes in. I am authorized to pay you and your organization the sum of three million dollars in exchange for your protection of General Tobutu until after the elections are held. Once elected, the general plans to establish his own handpicked palace guard, revamp the military, and rid the country of the Communists and the radicals. Perhaps, after a few months, we can work out an arrangement for WISCO to provide the necessary cadre to train a security force for the new president. However, for now, our main concern is keeping the man alive long enough to win that election. That is why I am here, Mr. Richards. I need to know if WISCO will take the contract."

Richards glanced briefly at York, then back to Hayes. "I'm certain you have people within your own organization who could handle this, Mr. Hayes, and a hell of a lot cheaper. Would you mind telling us why you prefer WISCO to provide the necessary security?"

Hayes would have been disappointed had Richards not asked that question. It was the sign of a thoughtful commander who did not lightly commit his men to a place where others refused to go—not without asking why. "Of course, Mr. Richards. Your firm is in no way affiliated with any branch or department of the government; therefore, General Tobutu's opponents cannot say that he is merely a lackey to the West, under the protection of CIA or any other American intelligence organization."

Richards nodded his understanding. It was a good point. One that Julius Keino would be quick to utilize if Hayes sent his men along with Tobutu. "When will you need an answer, Mr. Hayes?"

"General Tobutu is presently under our protection at a villa in Puerto Rico. He is anxious to return to Zimbabwe as soon as possible in order to begin his political rallies. He wishes to cover as much of the country as he can before election day. Therefore, I will need your answer within the next twenty-four hours, Mr. Richards. I am sure you can appreciate the time factor involved."

Richards nodded that he fully understood. Standing up, he said, "I certainly do, sir, just as I am certain you can understand that we cannot give you an immediate answer. We will need to run a feasibility evaluation of the situation, the area, and the participants that are involved. Should we decide that we can positively guarantee the safety of the client, we will begin a computer search of our field agents and select the proper number of personnel with the necessary skills and background to back that guarantee. I can assure you, Mr. Hayes, for three million dollars, General Tobutu and his benefactors will receive only the best that WISCO has to offer."

Hayes rose to his feet, as did Randy York. "I'm sure they will, Mr. Richards." Removing a business card from his jacket, Hayes handed it to York. It read, "Los Angeles Import/Export Unlimited." There were no names on the card, only a local number in the right-hand corner. "Once you have arrived at your decision, gentlemen, I can be reached at this number. I will remain in L.A. until I receive your answer. Now, I see you have much to do. So I'll be on my way."

Richards came from behind his desk, shook the CIA director's hand, and walked him to the door. York opened the door for the men and followed them out into the corridor. Hayes paused a moment, then asked, "Colonel Richards, there were a couple of things I was meaning to ask you. Would you mind?"

"Not at all, sir," said Richards, as York hesitated in pushing the elevator button to open the doors.

"Well, sir, when I arrived, I couldn't help but notice that once a vehicle enters your underground area they pass through a tunnel and directly beneath this building. Now, far be it for me to make a negative observation to someone with your knowledge of terrorism, but I couldn't help but think of the effect a car bomb would have were it to be detonated in that parking area. It could likely bring this entire building down."

Richards glanced at York, then back to Hayes, as Randy York muttered, "I'll be damned."

"You'll have to pardon Mr. York, sir. Prior to your arrival, I made a little bet with him that before you left, you would ask that very question. Let me assure you, Mr. Hayes, had your vehicle been carrying an explosive device, you would not be standing here right now. The tunnel you entered is actually a steel-and-marble-reinforced bomb containment area. You may not have noticed the colorful pinstripes running along the wall, but those are not merely colorful lines. They are sets of microscopic fibers that omit a variety of ultrahigh-frequency signals capable of detonating any explosive device currently known to man. There are two infrared sensors on the wall at the entrance capable of detecting explosive compounds. Once detected, a steel-plated shield is activated, coming up out of the floor, and sealing the entrance. That way, any blast will not exit out onto the streets, killing innocent pedestrians or drivers. The car advances ten yards—the signals trigger the device, and the terrorist threat is eliminated."

"Amazing," uttered Hayes, feeling like a total ass for having thought he had found a flaw in WISCO's security.

"And your second question, sir," asked Richards.

Hayes hesitated a moment. He wasn't sure he wanted to know the answer to his next question, but he asked anyway. "Yes, it has to do with your identification procedures downstairs. You are using the heat-print image mimeography computer system. Now, I know it's a damn good system. We use it ourselves. However, in order to cross-reference an image, you have to have an original print with which to cross-reference. My question, Mr. Richards, is, just how in the hell did you manage to get my fingerprints?"

Richards smiled, then looked down at the carpet for a moment. "Mr. Hayes, I'm afraid we'll have to pass on that one. Suffice it to say that if the President of the United States appeared at that block house downstairs, my people could run the exact same check on him. You see, sir, when you run a business where the minimum charge for services is one million dollars, and you have had that business for a number of years, you can afford the most expensive systems in the world or, as in our case, have one specially designed and manned by those that created it. However, I'm afraid I have already said more than I had intended. So, if you have no other questions, Mr. Hayes, Mr. York and I will begin work on your request."

The three men shook hands again and Hayes stepped into the elevator. The door closed and the music began again. Hayes was amazed by the coolness of the two men who ran WISCO. They were definitely professionals. If they were the standard by which the men they employed operated in the field, General Tobutu was going to be as safe in Zimbabwe as he had been in his mother's womb.

He exited the elevator. The guards nodded politely as he made his way to the limousine. The driver stood, holding the rear door open for the director, and asked, "Do you think they can handle the job, sir?"

Hayes paused as he looked back at the block house and the brightly colored pinstripes along the far tunnel wall, before he said, "Handle it! Hell, son, I have a feeling that this outfit could take over the whole damn country if they set their mind to it."

Randy York followed his partner back into his office. Suzie looked up from her typing. There was a stern look on the faces of her employers as they walked hurriedly past her into Erin Richard's office and closed the door. It was a look she had seen before. A look that signaled the beginning of an extensive operation that would involve more than the usual element of risk. A sudden chill came over her as she returned to her typing. It was a reaction the young woman experienced at the beginning of each new operation—a chill brought about by the thought that maybe this time, Randy York might be one of those going out as a field operative. How would she stop him if he did decide to go? How would she deal with the vast emptiness of her bed without Randy's strong, warm body to snuggle against in the night? What if he didn't come back?

Closing her eyes for a moment in an attempt to put that thought out of her mind, she managed only to set it aside for the time being and resume her typing. They would discuss it tonight.

Richards sat down behind his desk and made a phone call downstairs while York went to the east wall of the office and pressed a button next to the portable bar set against the wall. Two mahogany panels slid aside to reveal a huge, six-foot-by-six-foot television monitor screen. Located at the center base of the screen was a computer keyboard. York flipped the computer switch to activate the screen and typed in the words, "Africa . . . focus key . . . Zimbabwe."

Within seconds a three-dimensional color picture of Zimbabwe appeared on the monitor. Roads, lakes, rivers, and mountain ranges stood out in striking color. Bright red numbers at the high relief portions of the mountains identified the average altitude of the mountain ranges. An inset at the bottom right-hand corner of the screen provided the normal day/night temperature and expected rainfall for the current month.

York leaned forward and typed in the word "Harare"—the new designated name for the capital, formally known as Salisbury. The monitor went black for a second; then another color picture came on the screen. This one was an overhead view of the capital and the surrounding areas of the capital city. The satellite picture was so clear that, selecting a point anywhere on the map York could magnify that area until he could read the headlines on the front page of a newspaper being held by a man on the street. The new age of modern technology had indeed enhanced the world of military intelligence capabilities.

While York set up the screen, Richards talked on the phone to his computer chief located on the fifth floor. He wanted all current data on Zimbabwe, as well as the present components of the political factions and leaders that were active in the area. He also wanted a scan of all WISCO personnel with past background experience in the region. Once the information was ready, the chief was to bring it immediately to Richards's office.

Richards joined York at the map. Scanning the picture of the city, he asked, "How old is this shot?"

York pressed a computer key and a date/time group message appeared in the lower left corner. "Sat-1

WISCO uplink—0745 Hrs/10 Sept. '90."

Richards read the data, then said, "Five days old, Randy. Better have our boys schedule a series of update shots on Sat-One's next pass. We're going to need new updates every twenty-four hours if we decide to go with this thing."

"Roger, I agree. What's your initial gut feeling about this one, Erin?" asked York.

"Africa has always been a messy business, Randy. The man who tagged it the dark continent knew what he was talking about. Hell, a majority of the Africans hate the white man's guts, but even those poor bastards don't deserve to be ruled by a butcher like Julius Keino. For that reason alone, I think we should go with it." Randy York nodded in agreement.

CHAPTER TWO

Julius Keino sat on a bar stool in the far corner of the room and watched in silence as an electrical cattle prod was shoved against the fourteen-year-old black boy's testicles. An anguished look of pure pain instantly shot across the youth's face. His frail young body jerked violently. His mouth flew open wide, but no sound came forth. A second rapid shot, another jerk, and the boy's head fell forward. He had mercifully lost consciousness. The huge black man holding the instrument of torture looked back over his shoulder in Keino's direction.

Clasping a cigarette between his thumb and index finger, Russian style, Keino nodded toward the bucket of water sitting near the chair to which the boy had been securely tied. Setting aside the cattle prod, the big man grabbed up the bucket of water, stepped back, and threw its contents in the boy's face. Tossing the empty bucket into a corner, he recovered the prod and moved toward the lad.

The boy stirred slightly. A low moan escaped through split lips as he tried in vain to lift his badly battered face. His tormentor reached out with a burly hand, grasped a handful of hair and yanked the boy's head up. It was not a pretty sight. The boy's face was badly swollen. His nose, crooked and smashed to one side, was obviously broken. His right eye had received so many blows that white, glimmering bone now showed where an eyebrow should have been. Releasing the boy's hair, the big man turned to Keino. Placing his huge hands on his hips, he spoke in broken English. "I don't think maybe he take much more, Keino."

Julius Keino crossed one leg over the other and leaned back against the bar. Keino was not a big man. He stood only five-foot-nine and was of normal build, although he was thinner now from his years in the white man's prison in South Africa. His face was more bronze than black. A vivid, pink-brown scar ran the length of his nose on the left side, the result of having a knife inserted up his nostril and sliced wide open out the side during one of the many interrogations he himself had been subjected to over the years.

As he drew heavily on his cigarette its reddish glow was reflected in his coal black eyes—cruel, sadistic eyes that appeared to radiate hatred and evil. Dropping the cigarette to the floor, Keino leaned forward, and in a low yet threatening tone asked, "Have you become a man of medicine since I have been in prison, Sebota?"

The big man named Sebota raised an arm and wiped the small rivers of sweat from his face. The night was excessively hot, and he had nearly overworked himself in the past hour beating on the boy.

"No, Keino. I mean only to tell you—I no think he will live if I beat more on him. He die—then we no find out nothing you want to know. Maybe by morning, he want to talk to us plenty."

"Do you actually believe that, Sebota?" asked Keino with a smirk.

Sebota glanced down at the limp body of the young boy. He was a strong lad. Sebota had seen few grown men who could have endured the beating he had administered, let alone a boy of fourteen. Looking back to Keino, he meekly replied, "No, Keino. He would die before he tell on his friends."

Keino slid off the bar stool. Crossing the room, he stopped beside the chair, "You are correct, my friend. So be it."

Before Sebota could move out of the way, Keino pulled a pistol from behind his back and shot the boy through the head. Blood and parts of brain tissue splattered across Sebota's chest. The big man's first instinct was to yell out at the killer, but the depraved look in Keino's eyes quickly extinguished the thought.

Sliding the pistol back into place in his belt at the small of his back, Keino began to walk to the door, "Come. He was but one. There are others who are part of the secret coalition that are preparing for General Tobutu's return. Not all of them will be as stubborn as this one. Someone will tell us who the organizers of that coalition are. I want them out of the way before I start my campaign. Those who worked to set me free do not see the old general as a threat, but why take chances? When we find these 'leaders' they will all wish that their deaths would come as quickly as did that of the boy. Let's go."

Sebota picked up the tattered shirt that he had torn from the dead boy's body at the beginning of the interrogation. Following Keino to the door, Sebota used the shirt to wipe the blood and brains from his chest and tossed it to the floor as he walked out the door. Julius Keino had been out of prison less than twenty-four hours, and already the killing had begun.

The two founders of WISCO were both talking on the phones when Suzie entered the room carrying the computer readouts that Erin Richards had requested earlier in the day. She placed them on her boss's desk, smiled at Randy York, and glanced at her watch questioningly as she turned to leave the room. The handsome ex-Green Beret flashed her a wink and nodded in the affirmative as she passed his desk. The move was Suzie's discreet way of confirming whether or not they were still going out to dinner tonight. His silent reply brought a sparkle to her eyes. Their relationship had been going on for six months now. For Suzie, it was true love. She had dated lots of men, but none as kind, considerate, and thoughtful as Randy York. He was handsome, intelligent, and a man who possessed unbelievable stamina in the art of making love. He never failed to leave her totally satisfied. Anticipation of that face brought a sparkle to her eyes as she quietly closed the door on her way out.

"Yes, Dibó," said Richards to his South African contact over the phone, "We're going to need weapons compatible with a political bodyguard scenario. Preferably, 9-mm Berettas with shoulder holsters. Figure ten handguns with four magazines each. What do you have on hand in the way of automatic weapons systems for backup?"

Richards could hear a slight crackling over the line as Francois Dibó made adjustments on the secure-voice telephone at his end. He then replied, "Erin, I think we may have just the thing for you. The Israelis came out with a neat little item called a Mini-Uzi—cyclic rate of fire just under one thousand rounds per minute. Small and compact, it allows for three-to-four-round bursts; and with the twenty-round magazine, it is easily concealed. It also comes with a longer box-type magazine that gives you a thirty-two-round capability, Erin; but, it makes it harder to conceal. I've also got some .45 Acp-Mac-10s and 9-mm Colbray M-11s with twenty or thirty-two round capability. They are all pretty good weapons for that type situation, Erin. It just depends on what you want."

Richards noted the weapons on a notepad in front of him, before he asked, "What about heavy stuff?"

"Same story, Erin. We've got Colt, AR-15s, M-16A2s, Beretta AR-70s, H&K Model 91s, AK-50s, and MP-5s. You name it, my friend. If I don't have it—I can get it for you on twenty-four hours notice." Dibó paused for a moment, as he said, "Sounds like you might be doing a little heavy-duty business in our general vicinity, Erin. Your politician anybody I know?"

Richards leaned back in his chair; and, for a moment considered informing his old French friend of Tobutu's impending return to Zimbabwe; however, he thought better of it. Not that he didn't trust Dibó. It would be at least a week before the general would be in the country. Richards saw no sense in stirring up a lot of excitement so far in advance. There would be enough of that once Tobutu stepped off the plane in Zimbabwe. Rather than giving an answer, Richards asked a question of his own. "Dibó, what's the story on Julius Keino? I hear you people are letting that butcher go pretty soon."

The other end of the line went silent. For a second, Richards thought perhaps they had been disconnected. When Francois finally did speak, it was with a bitter tone that only one who had seen Keino's massacre could express.

"That bastard! We should have hung him the minute he fell into our hands. Your information is partially correct, my friend. Our government has already effected the release of the son-of-a-bitch, two days ago, to be precise. The prime minister hasn't released the news, yet. They know the uproar it will cause among the whites in Africa when they do. They felt it wise to have Keino out of the country before the announcement. That way, if anybody kills the bastard, it won't be on South African soil. And you can bet, if his removal hadn't been carried out in secret, every South African between here and Zimbabwe would have been lying in ambush for his black ass. My sources say they managed to sneak him across the border two nights ago. No telling what the asshole is up to now."

This new information heightened Richards's concern. The CIA boys were apparently lagging in their intelligence reports. Even the director of the CIA didn't know Keino had already been released—or did he?

"Erin, you still there, Erin?" asked Francois.

"Uh . . . yes, Francois, sorry. I was just thinking about something."

"No problem, Erin. Look here—you wouldn't happen to be going after Julius Keino would you?" asked Dibó in a wishful voice.

"No, Francois, it's something totally different this trip. But you can never tell from which direction trouble may come. This news of Keino's release could be very useful to us. I thank you."

Francois gave a pleasant laugh, then said, "Well, my old friend, if the little bastard should cross your path anytime during your visit to our continent, you and WISCO could surely establish national hero status in South Africa by blowing his bloody brains out— quite by accident, of course."

"Of course," replied Richards with a smile. "Who knows? You may just get your wish." Glancing at his watch, Richards said, "Listen, Francois, I have to go. It sounds like you have just the equipment we will need. Of course, weapons selection will be up to the leader of the WISCO security team. If he has any special request, I'll see to it that you have plenty of lead time for procurement. My secretary will fax a message to Zurich authorizing a transfer of twenty-five thousand dollars to your account as a retainer. We'll notify you twenty-four hours before departure as to when and where we will take delivery of the merchandise."

"That will be fine, Erin. I'll start on this matter this afternoon. Until then, goodbye, my friend."

Richards switched off the secure-voice telephone system and hung up the receiver. Across the room, Randy York was finalizing the transportation plans for the movement of General Tobutu and the security team to Zimbabwe. York had already reached an agreement on the price required for a chartered 707 jet. A DC-10 would have been much cheaper, but the limited range of that aircraft would require a stopover for refueling—something that was not desired. The 707 could make it straight to Zimbabwe on a full load. Pilots and navigators would not be required by the airline; WISCO had its own crew.

York jotted down the account number of the airline and informed them that a check in the amount requested would be at their bank before today's close of business. Hanging up the phone, he did some quick adding up of the figures: the charter, the fuel, and the cost of the crew. Tossing his pen aside, he stared across at Richards and said, "Well, that's not too bad, I suppose—thirty-three thousand dollars for the trip one-way, with a retainer of twenty thousand dollars toward insurance on the plane, in case something unfortunate should happen to their aircraft."

The head of WISCO did not act as though he had heard York's comment. Standing, York walked across the room. It was apparent that Richards was deep in thought. Easing himself down into the chair next to the desk, York asked, "Something wrong, Erin?"

Glancing up at his partner with a hint of suspicion in his eyes, he replied, "Francois says they moved Keino out of South Africa and across the border over forty-eight hours ago."

York slumped back in his chair with a pained expression on his face. "Shit!"

"Exactly," said Richards, leaning forward and pushing the computer readouts that lay in front of him across the desk to York. "If you liked that little piece of news, Randy, then you're going to love this. Look who our multimillion-dollar computer selected as the best man for this job."

York sat up and turned the readout sheets toward himself. Seeing the name at the top of the sheet, he again whispered, "Shit."

Richards couldn't help but grin as he said, "Major, we're going to have to see if we can't do something to enhance your vocabulary."

York was still staring at the name. Beside it were the words, "Inoperative." Leaning back in his chair, Randy said, "You know he won't take the job, don't you? Hell, he just got married less than ten months ago. After losing Buck Buchanan during that Randolph business in Laos last year, he said he was through with this kind of work—and I believe him, Erin. He and Buck were like brothers. That really took a lot out of him."

Richards pondered that statement for a moment. What York said was true. The Randolph contract had been a difficult one. Although a successful operation, it had proven very costly in terms of lives lost. Normally, Richards would have agreed with York's evaluation; however, there was an element involved here which his partner was not aware of, nor any computer could note on a piece of paper. The man in question for this contract owed his life to General Tobutu—that was the kind of debt an ex-Green Beret didn't forget.

Pulling the readout back in front of him, Richards circled the name in red pencil as he said, "Randy, I'm going to tell you a story. When I'm finished, I

want you to fly out to Fayetteville, North Carolina.
This is not the kind of offer I want made over the
phone. If I know our boy as well as I think I do,
and I should—he ran the hottest damn Blue Light
Team on the Delta Force—once he is made aware
of the players involved, he'll be flying back here
with you."

It was clear from York's expression that he did not
share his partner's view. "I'm not so sure, Erin. His
wife Sharon will pitch a fit over this. You can count
on it."

Erin smiled as he thought of the well-built little
blonde who had managed to snare one of his best
operatives. "I'm sure she will, Randy. But, she put up
with his comings and goings for twenty years before
she finally married him. It isn't like it would be a new
experience."

"Yeah, Erin, but she always knew that Buck was
with him and would be covering his back."

The smile faded from Erin's face. Again, York had
spoken the truth. A man could harden himself to the
realities of death in this high-risk business, but the loss
of a friend who you had known, loved, and worked
with all your career could shatter that self-imposed
hardness into a thousand pieces. Even the strongest
of men are vulnerable if they lack the ability to feel
or cry, unashamed, at the loss of a friend. The day
Buck died, there had been plenty of that. Equally so,
one could not dwell on the past. What was done, was
done, and could not be changed. And a man whose
entire life had been guided by the profession of arms
and who possessed a natural ability in the art of war
could not suppress for long the desire to do what he

knew he did best. The man at the top of this list was just such a man.

Reaching across his desk, Richards pressed a button on his intercom. "Susan, call the airlines and book Mr. York for a round-trip flight to Fayetteville, North Carolina. He'll be leaving tonight. Then get in contact with the Military Retired Pay Division in Indianapolis, Indiana. Ask to speak to Mr. Charles Verneer, he's the head of the department. Tell him that Erin Richards needs the current address of retired Sergeant Major Paul Stryker."

CHAPTER THREE

Sharon Stryker squeezed some suntan lotion into her hands, set the bottle aside, leaned forward, and began to rub it onto the broad shoulders of her husband Paul. She smiled to herself when she heard him give a soft moan of contentment as her small hands moved in a slow, circular motion.

Paul Stryker lay on his stomach, his six-foot-four frame stretched out on a beach towel. His head rested on crossed arms. His sky blue eyes closed against the brilliant sun that promised another warm North Carolina day.

Applying more cream, Sharon moved her hands down the small of his back. She could feel the hardened, cordlike muscles relax and give way to her gentle touch. She rubbed harder as she stared out across the rolling blue waters of the ocean. A sailboat bobbed its way along the distant horizon. It was so peaceful here, and in that peace, Sharon Stryker stole a moment to reflect on how, after twenty-two years, she had finally managed to arrive at this time and place with the man she had always loved.

It was like a dream come true. But it had not been an easy journey. She had met Paul Stryker over twenty-one years ago. Then a junior at the University of North Carolina, she had spent the summer helping her father operate the Rustic Lounge, a bar and nightclub that he had purchased after retiring from the army with thirty years of service behind him. She could still remember the very first day the tall, good-looking Green Beret walked into the bar and into her life. His smile and dazzling blue eyes had practically melted her on the spot. Charlie, her father, immediately saw the attraction between the two. It delighted him, yet it sparked concern. From what her father knew of Sergeant Paul Stryker, he was the perfect example of the clean-cut, all-American boy, and the old retired sergeant major liked him. But, this was the time of the Vietnam War and the Green Beret that Stryker wore so proudly left little doubt in Charlie's mind where Stryker would be going soon. He didn't object to the courtship, but he didn't encourage it.

By the end of that summer the whirlwind romance was teetering on the verge of marriage. Then the orders came. Charlie offered to pull a few strings and call in some favors still owed, to get Paul's orders changed, but Stryker wouldn't allow it. Feeling hurt and rejected, Sharon threw her engagement ring at Stryker and stormed out of the club. That had been twenty-two years ago.

Their lives had taken different paths. Paul had never married. His natural ability at warfare gained him notoriety and fame throughout the military community.

His reputation was built on the success of complicated operations and mission achievements that spanned the world. Sharon, on the other hand, had been married and divorced twice. She had raised two fine children and put them both through college. In all those years, she never forgot Paul Stryker. The Green Beret had sparked a fire within her unlike any other man. Following her father's death, she had taken over the management of the Rustic. There were constant reminders of Paul as Green Berets passing through talked of Stryker's latest exploits in Southeast Asia, Central America, the Middle East, and a hundred other places where war and violence were the order of the day. Only a year ago she had experienced a moment of panic when it was rumored that Stryker had been killed in Africa. Frantic phone calls to old friends of her father proved the rumors false.

One month after that, Paul Stryker walked into the Rustic and back into her life. Older, but just as ruggedly handsome as ever, the tall man rekindled that fire within her with a mere smile. Sharon had hoped that he had finally reached an age where he was ready to settle down, but any illusion of that vanished with the appearance of Colonel Richards and Randy York.

Even now, Paul spoke very little of what had happened only ten short months ago. She had never pressed the matter. All she knew for sure was that the operation engineered by Erin Richards and the people of WISCO had resulted in the death of Buck Buchanan, a longtime friend and a man who was practically a brother to Paul Stryker. That loss had brought about a change in Paul's attitude toward wars and world unrest. He was a man who had spent over half of his life fighting other people's wars, from the snowcapped mountains of Afghanistan to the sweltering heat of the jungles of the Philippines and what good had it done? Nothing had been accomplished—only friends lost.

"Hey, what happened to the magic fingers?" asked Stryker, sleepily.

Sharon suddenly realized she had been so deep in thoughts of the past that her hands had stopped moving on Paul's back. Her fingers rested on the long pink scar along her lover's side. It was the latest of many that covered his body. Grabbing up the bottle, she squeezed a long stream down his back as she jokingly said, "Sorry, ol' master Paul. I fear I doest daydream in your presence."

Paul laughed as he shifted his head on his arms and snickered, "I'll forgive you this time, but don't let it happen again."

Rubbing his back again, she replied, "This is going to cost you, brother."

"Oh, really!" he laughed again. "Well, we better negotiate before you go any farther. I may not want to pay your price."

Sharon straddled the back of his legs. Leaning forward, she pressed harder on his back, "Oh, is that so? You think you can get a better deal somewhere else, do you?"

The brush of her smooth legs against his as she rocked back and forth on his body began to excite him. In a sheepish tone, he said, "Well, I don't know for sure, but there's a damn good-looking redhead who just moved in down the beach. From what the locals tell me, she just might appreciate a little exchange of body rubs."

Sliding back on his legs, Sharon slapped him hard on the butt. "Oh yeah!" Glancing down between his legs, she saw that her husband was definitely aroused by her movements. Big hands and big feet were not the only big things Paul Stryker possessed. Leaning forward and softening her tone, she pressed her bikini-held breasts hard against his bare back and purred, "Would you really like to go play in the sand with the little redheaded girl, darling?"

Stryker, his eyes still closed, grinned as he said, "Might prove interesting."

Sharon quickly sat upright. Her hand shot between his legs. Her hand wrapped around his manhood and she pulled slightly as she giggled, "Okay then! But you'll have to leave your toys at home."

"Oh, shit!" yelled Stryker, struggling to roll over. "Damn, Sharon, you're going to pull the damn thing off."

They were still wrestling in the sand and laughing when a shadow fell over them. They paused and looked up to see Randy York standing over them. He wore a bright yellow polo shirt and white shorts with sneakers, and he would not have seemed out of place were it not for the briefcase he held in his hand.

"Sorry to interrupt such an intimate moment, but I need to talk to you, Paul."

The laughter suddenly stopped. "Intimate moment," thought Sharon, as she realized that she had pulled Paul's swimsuit halfway off and still had her hand wrapped tightly around his pulsating erection. Her hand shot back as if she had touched a hot stove. A crimson blush flowed into her cheeks as she looked down at the sand.

Seeing the blush spread about her face, Paul laughed heartily as he pulled his trunks back up and said, "Now see, you got caught with your hands in the cookie jar, didn't you honey?"

"Screw you, Stryker," she muttered under her breath. Paul sat up. Brushing the sand from his arms and standing up, Stryker said, "Sorry, honey, but I don't think Randy's into that voyeur thing."

Sharon didn't bother to raise her head. Scooping up a pile of sand in her hands, she said, "Nothing personal, Mr. York, but I had hoped we would never see you again."

"Now, Sharon, that's not very neighborly of you. Randy could be here just for a visit," said Paul, offering his hand to help his wife up.

Sharon clasped Paul's hand and pulled herself up. Glancing at the briefcase in York's hand as she brushed the sand from her attractive legs, she replied, "No, I don't think so, Paul. It's business, isn't it, Mr. York?" Barely able to contain the anxiety in her voice, she continued, "I think I'll go for a walk, Paul. I wouldn't want to hear this, even if I could."

Stryker reached out to her, but she pushed his hand away. The joy and smiles of a moment before were gone. Picking up the towel, she wrapped it around her shoulders and walked away.

"Sorry, Paul, guess I should have called first," said York.

Paul watched his wife walk along the water's edge with her head down. Her feet were kicking at the sand and water. Sharon was an attractive woman at forty-five and could still turn more than a few heads in her direction.

"That's okay, Randy. She'll get over it after she's walked awhile. Come on, we'll go up to the house, and I'll buy you a drink."

Stryker refrained from comment about the briefcase or the purpose of York's visit until after he had prepared the drinks and directed his guest out onto the deck overlooking the beach. Settling into a wicker chair, Paul sipped at his Jack Daniel's and ice, then asked, "How's the colonel doing?"

Rotating the drink in his hand, Randy forced a smile and answered, "Fine, Paul. Just fine."

There was a moment of strained silence between the two men as each tipped their glasses and stared out across the ocean. Taking a final sip of his drink, Paul placed the glass on the table and leaned back in his chair. Clasping his hands in front of him, Paul said, "Okay, Randy, let's have it. You didn't come all the way from L.A. just to catch Sharon holding my dick in her hand. What's up?"

Randy set his glass down, opened the briefcase, and removed the computer readout sheets on selected personnel. He slid them over in front of Stryker. "To keep it simple, Paul, WISCO has a million-dollar computer that says you're the best man for a contract we have just acquired. That's why I'm here."

Stryker pulled the papers into his lap and began to read.

Stryker, Paul, W. Age: 45. Height: 6'4". Weight: 220. Retired Sergeant Major—U.S. Army (Special Forces). Awards: Distinguished Service Cross, two Silver Stars, four Bronze Stars for Valor, four Purple Hearts. Combat

History: Three tours: Republic of Vietnam.
Recon Team Leader, MACV-SOG, Command
and Control North. Detached Special Duty with
Central Intelligence Agency Laos, 1972–1974
(Wounded twice—no awards) Training Advisor,
Rhodesian Selous Scouts, Counterterrorist Unit,
1974–1976 (Wounded '76—no award) Delta
Force Team Sergeant. Active during Iranian
Rescue Mission (Desert One) Grenada Invasion
(Urgent Fury) Retired U.S. Military, 1984. Rank
of Sergeant Major. Freelance contract work for
CIA; Afghanistan—1985; El Salvador—1986;
Angola, Africa—1987.

Led successful independent mission (Privately
funded) into Laos for rescue of American civilian personnel captured by Laotian bandits.

Present status: Inactive.

NOTHING FOLLOWS

Stryker tossed the paper onto the table. "Hell, Randy,
that's pretty impressive, but I'm afraid your million-
dollar Tinker toy wasted its time. That computer might
tell you boys I'm your man, but I've got a twenty-dollar
marriage license that says your computer is wrong."

York picked up his glass, leaned back in his chair,
and said, "That's what I told the colonel before he
booked my flight out here."

Stryker seemed surprised by York's comment.

"But, he sent you anyway. Why, Randy? I spent
too many years working for that old man to know he
doesn't place his bets unless he's certain of a return
on his investment. He's got a hole card somewhere in
this deal. What is it, Randy?"

A grin crossed York's face as he laughed and said, "Jesus, are you sure you and the colonel aren't father and son? I mean, you both seem to think exactly alike."

"Just where is this job, Randy?" asked Paul.

"Zimbabwe."

"Zimbabwe, my ass!" said Stryker with a hint of bitterness, "It's still Rhodesia as far as I'm concerned. Stupid fuckers think they can change the name of a country and all the problems will somehow go away. Well, they were wrong, weren't they? You bet your ass they were. The terrorists got what they wanted, thanks to a damn bunch of bleeding-heart liberals who shouted loud enough and long enough until they got their way. Then, the bastards moved on down the road to lay that same crap on South Africa. Of course, Rhodesia went to hell in a hand basket after that. The economy went to shit. The people were starving, and naturally, every fucking body had a damn rifle so it was time to settle old tribal feuds—damn blacks were killing each other by the thousands, but the liberals didn't want to hear about that. That was considered an internal matter and no concern of theirs. Zimbabwe, my ass! It's just too fucking bad we couldn't drag all those bleeding hearts back there at gunpoint and make them live in that hell hole they created for a year or so. That would have provided them with a whole new perspective on their views of African interference."

Stryker paused from his hell fire and damnation speech long enough to take a drink before asking, "Is that why your computer picked me, Randy? Because I had those two years in the bush with the Selous Scouts?"

York cocked a foot on the deck railing and rocked back in his chair. "I would say that played a major part in it, but the rest of the readout is equally impressive, Paul. I'd say it was a combination of both."

Looking out along the beach for some sign of Sharon, Stryker said, "Last I heard, Randy, you boys had Pop Everson working for you. Hell, that guy worked for the CIA in Rhodesia for so damn long, people thought he was born and raised there. He knows that country ten times better than I do. Why didn't your computer pick him for this deal?"

"Pop's dead, Paul."

Stryker's head snapped around toward York with a hurt look in his eyes. "When?"

"About a month ago in El Salvador," replied York, slowly running his finger around the rim of his glass. "Chopper was shot down. Fucking guerrillas got to the crash site before the El Sal troops. They shot Pop and the pilots to pieces while they were crawling out of the wreckage."

Stryker lowered his head. With remorse in his voice, he said, "Damn, I hate to hear that. Pop taught me everything I know about Rhodesia. Even saved my ass once when a bunch of us were captured by guerrillas. Pop knew the leader of the group that was holding us. He came walkin' in as bold as you please, and within an hour had talked the commander into releasing us. Damnedest thing I ever saw. We just knew they were going to cut us up into little pieces before Pop showed up. How he pulled that off, I'll never know."

"Yeah," said York, "the colonel told me about that. You happen to remember the name of that guerrilla leader that Pop talked to, Paul?"

Stryker looked up at York. "Hell, yes, I do. When you've got over fifty black guerrillas standing around sharpening up their knives to play a little afternoon game of cut and slash on your white ass, you take notice of things like that. I don't mind telling you, the guy's decision wasn't really appreciated by a few of those boys. The commander had to shoot a couple of 'em to get his point across. Damn good thing he did, too; otherwise, they would have been peeling our skin off for days."

"What was the guy's name, Paul?"

"Tobutu, Colonel Moise Tobutu. I understand they made him a general just before the war ended."

York dropped his foot from the railing. Removing a photo from the briefcase, he slid it across the table to Stryker. "Is that your boy, Tobutu?"

Stryker stared down at the smiling black face of the man adorned in full military dress uniform with a mountain of medals along the side. The gleaming white teeth and lively eyes were the same as Paul remembered from that day.

"Yeah, that's Tobutu. Not a bad guy really. He definitely believed in what he was fighting for, I can tell you that. Matter of fact, he was the only one out of the whole damn bunch we were fighting in those days that the Rhodesians had a sense of respect for. He didn't mistreat his prisoners, and if he gave his word about anything, you could take it to the bank. All in all, not a damn bad guy for a guerrilla leader. What are you doing with his picture, Randy? Is Tobutu involved in this deal?"

York nodded. He told Stryker the story of what had happened to Tobutu's family following the war. He told of his son's going to college and the desire of the people for Tobutu to return to Zimbabwe for the elections. The blacks, as well as the few remaining whites, believed the general to be their last hope for saving the country.

Stryker listened intently to every detail. When the name Julius Keino came up, Stryker leaped to his feet, fired off a string of curse words, and fixed them both another drink, all the while, making some rather uncomplimentary remarks about not only Keino, but the man's mother, as well. Setting the fresh drink in front of York allowed Stryker to finish his appraisal of Keino before he said, "Okay, Paul. You see what we have here is an honest man who wants to return to his country and his people and do what he can to restore it to the greatness it once knew. In order to do that, he has to be elected next month."

"You mean he has to be kept alive long enough to be elected, don't you?" replied Stryker.

"Exactly, Paul. That's why we need someone to head up a team that can cover Tobutu while he runs his campaign. We're confident he can win by a landslide, as long as no one takes him down before the elections. That's where you come in. The computer says you're the best man to guarantee his safety."

Stryker stirred his drink with his finger. His eyes studied the rolling waves breaking against the shore. Tobutu was the colonel's hole card. The old bastard knew that Stryker owed the black general his life. He also knew that Stryker wouldn't allow the debt to go unpaid. Erin Richards ran his business with the same shrewdness that had endeared him to many during his days as commander of the Delta Force. Looking over at York, Stryker said, "There are never any guarantees in this business, Randy. Well, maybe one. I'll bet that sly old bastard who's your partner booked passage for two back to L.A., didn't he?"

York smiled. Digging around in his briefcase, he tossed two tickets across the table. "First class—aisle seats. Departure time, 0800 hours. The colonel said to let you know that if Sharon wanted to come along, we'll get another ticket, and she can fly out with us and spend some time in L.A. until you get back. We've got an estate near the ocean. She'd be more than welcome, Paul."

Stryker stood and walked to the railing. As he looked down the beach a flood of emotions ripped through him like a hot poker. He had made a lot of promises after Buck had died. Promises not only to Sharon, but to himself as well. For over twenty years he had been killing people or had people trying to kill him. He had sworn that he was finished with all of that. The money from the Randolph operation in Laos had set him up for life, but this wasn't about money. It was about an unpaid debt, a debt no amount of money could erase. This was a matter of obligation, respect, and honor. Richards had known that when he sent York to North Carolina. Stryker had no problem with that. The problem would be trying to convince Sharon of his obligation.

Randy York stood and moved to the railing. A slight breeze rustled through the trees nearby. Randy was well aware of the turmoil of decision that must be raging through Stryker at the moment. In his own way, York attempted to take some of the pressure off his old friend.

"Nice place you've got here, Paul. How much of this beachfront is yours?"

Seeing Sharon returning up the beach, Stryker answered, "All of it, Randy! Look, you're welcome to spend the night. We'll leave early in the morning. Now, if you'll excuse me. I have some explaining to do." Vaulting over the railing, Stryker walked out to the beach to meet his wife. They talked for a moment, kissed, then walked hand in hand along the shore. Stopping once, they stared at each other, hugged, and continued on until they were out of sight.

Placing his glass on the table, York gathered up his papers and the tickets. He put them in his briefcase, and walked through the house to the front door. He appreciated Stryker's offer, but he couldn't stand to hear a woman cry, and he had a good idea that there would be a lot of crying in this house before morning.

CHAPTER FOUR

Rutherford Hayes lifted his glass in a toast. "To WISCO, General Tobutu, and mission success. Hopefully, with an honest man in power, Zimbabwe will once again become the pearl of Africa."

"Here, here!" chanted Major York, tipping his glass to his lips. Erin Richards motioned his glass toward Paul Stryker. "To good luck and good fortune, Paul."

Stryker nodded his thanks and downed his champagne with a grimace. He hated the bitter-tasting crap, but it was the CIA director's party. Stryker would have preferred Jack on the rocks. The toast completed, the four men sat back down around the dining table. Hayes and Richards lit up cigars. Paul pulled a Marlboro from the pack inside his dinner jacket and lit it. York was the only member of the group who had never begun the habit of smoking.

"So, tell me, Paul. When would you like to begin the personnel selection for this operation?" asked Richards.

Stryker glanced down at his watch before saying, "In about one hour, sir."

Hayes gave a short laugh and grinned at Richards. "My, my. You were right, Colonel. Mr. Stryker is not a man who cares for idle time." Looking at Stryker, he continued, "Really, Mr. Stryker, General Tobutu will not be going anywhere for a few days. I would think you would allow yourself a little relaxation. After all, you've only been in L.A. a few hours, and I know that was a long flight today."

A waiter suddenly appeared and refilled Stryker's glass with more champagne; then he made his way around the table doing the same for the others. After the waiter departed, Stryker said, "No, Mr. Hayes. The relaxation begins when this thing is over and not until then. From what you have already told me, the elections are only a few weeks away. With Julius Keino running around loose over there, the sooner I get the general back into Zimbabwe the better. As far as working tonight is concerned, I find that by keeping myself busy, I don't have time to question the wisdom of my decision to be a participant."

Hayes cast a sideways glance at Richards as he looked back at Stryker. In a vain attempt to be tactful, Hayes said, "Excuse me, Mr. Stryker, but I was under the impression that you were wholeheartedly behind this operation. However, it would appear that you have certain doubts about this. Would you care to elaborate on your statement, sir?"

Stryker reached for his glass; then he thought of the awful taste the bitter grapes left in his mouth. Screw that. Waving the waiter over, he ordered a double Jack Daniel's on ice. Turning back to Hayes, he said, "Mr.

Hayes, let's just say that if it were any other man besides Moise Tobutu who was involved in this deal, Mother Stryker's little boy Paul would still be lying out on the beach in North Carolina getting his dick squeezed."

Again Hayes looked toward Richards. The colonel still showed no desire to enter the conversation. Choosing instead to sit back in his chair in silence, his eyes focused on the smoldering Cuban cigar that he rolled gently between his fingers, Randy York was equally silent.

"Well, then, Mr. Stryker," said Hayes, "since you apparently have doubts about your capability to see this thing through, perhaps it would be best for all concerned if we . . ."

"I didn't say that, Mr. Hayes," said Stryker sharply, cutting off the director. "I said, if it were any man but Tobutu, I would not be sitting here now. But that is not the case, is it? As far as my capabilities are concerned, I am sure that the minute the colonel gave you my name, your computers in Virginia began spitting out a stack of information on me to include my jockstrap size. I think the record speaks for itself, Mr. Hayes. You may have noted that I have done considerable work for your organization in the past, and neither Mr. Casey nor Mr. North ever asked for their money back." Stryker paused as the waiter brought his drink. "No, Mr. Hayes, I have no doubts that I owe General Tobutu a debt. I will repay that debt, sir. Have no doubts about that."

Hayes nodded his approval of the statement as Stryker downed the double Jack in one shot before sliding his chair back and standing.

"Now, if you gentlemen will excuse me, I'm afraid I am going to have to spirit Mr. York from your midst to help me run a readout on the potential personnel for tomorrow's interviews. Sorry, Randy, but I really do need to get started on this thing," said Stryker in an apologetic tone.

"No problem, Paul," replied York, downing his wine and rising to his feet. "Mr. Hayes, thank you for the dinner. Colonel, we'll see you both in the morning."

Hayes reached his hand out to Stryker. Paul grabbed it. The old man had a firm grip. "Thank you, Mr. Stryker."

Stryker smiled and released the director's hand as he and York left the dining room to head for the offices of WISCO. Hayes retrieved his glass and slumped back in his chair, "Rather impressive man you have there, Erin."

Richards blew a perfect smoke ring from his cigar as he replied, "Your predecessor and Ollie thought so."

"Yes, well, my predecessor wasn't much for the administrative side of this business. I'm sure there are a few missing chapters in Mr. Stryker's file."

Richards grinned. "Yeah, don't you just hate it when you spend all night reading a book only to find the final page missing."

Hayes returned the grin. Raising his glass, he said, "Yes, but I'm sure anything the CIA is missing can be provided by WISCO. To Mr. Stryker."

"To Mr. Stryker," replied Richards as the two glasses chimed together.

* * *

It was after midnight by the time the computer scan had been completed. A one-foot-high stack of printouts sat on the desk. Suzie flipped off the computer and collapsed in a nearby chair. Randy had called her before leaving the restaurant. Without her help, Paul and Randy would have been there all night.

York moved over to the chair next to her and flopped down, his eyes heavy, his body drained by jet lag. York didn't know how Stryker could do it. The man was on his second pot of coffee and already pulling the first sheet from the mountain of readout material they had accumulated over the last three hours.

Tilting his head slightly, York saw that Suzie was already asleep. They had gone two nights in a row without their normal passionate lovemaking. They had done that before, but never three nights in a row. Tonight would have to be chalked up as a new record—they were both too exhausted.

"I'll be damned!" said Stryker with a renewed enthusiasm from across the room. "Captain William P. McMillian."

"Wh . . . what?" said York, turning his head toward the desk while trying to focus his bloodshot eyes. If Stryker was tired, you couldn't prove it by the tone of his voice. He was as excited as a kid at Christmastime.

"Willy McMillian, Randy. Had one of the armored units of the Black Tigers in Rhodesia. His African troops loved the guy. They even made up a poem about him. Now, let's see, how did that thing go . . . oh yeah, 'Willy McMillian, the Scot who claimed to be from Finland, for his mother would shriek, and his father would howl if they knew that little Willy was doing all this killing and how—poor little Willy McMillian!' His father was a Catholic bishop, you know. God, this is perfect, and the first one off the stack, Randy. How 'bout that?"

Stryker looked up from the paper. Randy York's head was resting on Suzie's shoulder. They were both sound asleep. He stared at them for a long moment. A familiar pain went through him: the pain of loneliness, the pain of missing Sharon. Paul had told her of WISCO's offer to come to L.A., but she hadn't wanted to leave their home along the beach. It would be harder to wait out the long days and even longer nights until his return in a strange place. He understood that and had not pushed the matter further. This decision of his had been hard enough on her as it was.

Removing the last cigarette from his pack of Marlboros, Stryker lit it and refilled his coffee cup. Moving to the sleeping couple, Paul touched York gently on the shoulder. "Randy. Wake up, Randy."

York, still half asleep, raised his weary head. "Wha . . . what is it, Paul?"

"Listen ol' buddy, why don't you take Suzie home? I've got everything I need. No reason for you two to stick around. I'll leave a note for the colonel with the names of the men I want to interview, and tell him we'll be in by noon tomorrow, okay?" said Stryker.

Rubbing at his bloodshot eyes, York replied, "Are . . . are you sure, Paul. I . . . I can help you go through . . ."

Stryker patted him on the shoulder as he cut him off. "No, really, Randy, there's no need for that. Now come on, get Suzie up and you two get out of here.

I'll be through in a couple of hours."

York nodded. Shaking Suzie lightly, he leaned over, gave her a kiss on the cheek, and woke her up. Together they made their way out of the office and to the elevator. Pushing the button, York glanced back up the hall at Stryker, who was leaning against the doorway with his coffee cup in his hand. "You sure, Paul?" asked York once more.

"I'm sure, Randy—see you tomorrow."

The couple waved goodbye as they stepped into the elevator and the doors closed. Stryker returned to the desk and the stack of printouts. Picking up the one containing the information on William McMillian, he noted that the Scotsman was presently on leave in Panama and was due to return in one week. That did not present a problem. No interview would be necessary. McMillian could join them in Zimbabwe in a week. No need to screw up the guy's vacation. Transcribing those ideas on the paper, Stryker set it to the left of the pile and removed the next sheet.

Sheer, John, W. Age: twenty-three. Airborne, Ranger qualified. Six years active duty, United States Army. Highest rank held: Sergeant, E-5. Light and Heavy Weapons Specialist. 5/5 Language capability in Russian and French. Combat Experience: Limited. Grenada Invasion, Panama Invasion. Decorated for heroism in both operations. Applied for Delta Force selection June, 1988. Dismissed from training; low score, Land Orientation. Release from military duty before retest.

A smile formed along Stryker's lips as he read the reason for the young sergeant's dismissal from Delta training. He had seen those same remarks on his own records on his first attempt at Delta selection. They ran one of the toughest compass courses in the country. This kid, Sheer, didn't have anything to be ashamed of. A hell of a lot of good men had burned out on their first try for selection. He was in good company. That had nothing to do with Stryker's decision. The major factors were the age, and the limited combat experience. Going in balls to the wall during an invasion was one thing—protecting one man and shooting at selective targets in a crowd was a totally different ball game. Placing Sheer's record to the right of the stack, Stryker whispered to himself, "Maybe someday, son, but not today."

It was three in the morning by the time Stryker finished with the records. Not counting McMillian, he had selected thirty-one personnel for interviews. Of that number, he would select twenty for the job. Ten of whom would go in with Tobutu. The remaining ten would be flown to Johannesburg, South Africa, where they would remain on standby status as backup for the primary team under the command of Randy York.

The selection process would begin in nine hours. If all went as planned, Paul Stryker expected to have General Tobutu in Zimbabwe within the next seventy-two hours.

Placing the list of names on the colonel's desk, Stryker walked to the door and reached over to turn out the lights. His eyes came to rest on the telephone on Suzie's desk. For a moment he thought of calling Sharon, but, looking at his watch and remembering the time difference on the East Coast, he decided against it. It was a good bet that she had been up most of the night anyway worrying about him. By now, she would be asleep. He didn't want to disturb her. The sleeplessness she had gone through tonight would be but the first of many that would follow until this thing was over.

Turning out the lights, Paul Stryker made his way to the elevator. As he waited, the burden of responsibility that he had accepted now rested fully on his shoulders. It was an awesome responsibility, the placing of men's lives in danger, men who relied on his decisions and judgment. One wrong decision and someone could die. Added to the emotional pressures of having left Sharon alone and the long hours spent traveling to L.A., Paul Stryker suddenly realized how tired he really was. As the elevator doors opened, the ex-Green Beret's only thoughts were of a soft bed, a pillow, and sleep.

Office: Minister of Internal Affairs

Harare, Zimbabwe

Joshua Chihota, internal affairs minister of Zimbabwe, listened intently as, one by one, the deputy security commissioners of each territorial province provided their weekly reports on activities within their districts. Normally, these weekly meetings were routine, dealing primarily with criminal matters or tribal disputes, all of which Chihota usually ignored. However, this was the year of the elections and the minister's primary focus was now clearly on matters of civil unrest which might appear politically orchestrated.

Rumors that General Moise Tobutu might be returning to Zimbabwe as a candidate had been confirmed by the Zimbabwe Central Intelligence. His exact arrival date in-country was still not known. Hopefully, through the use of informants and village spies, the district commissioners could effectively gauge the strength of Tobutu's support across the country. Up until now all Chihota had been hearing were the same boring statistical breakdowns of criminal activity he had heard every week: rape up ten percent, theft twenty-five percent, and the usual unexplained murders and revenge killings that had plagued the country since the day of independence.

Forty-five minutes into the meeting and five commissioners later, Chihota knew no more about the status of Tobutu supporters than he had before the meeting. Irritated by the lack of air-conditioning sufficient to cool the overcrowded room and the obvious lack of information gathered on political matters by his commissioners, the minister raised his hand, interrupting the commissioner of Mutula Province. "Thank you, Mr. Naknoa—I see no need to proceed further. Please be seated."

The squat little African from Mutula expressed a sigh of relief that he had been relieved of his task. Sweating profusely, Naknoa returned to his seat.

Joshua Chihota wiped his brow with a silk handkerchief, then stood. His piercing black eyes surveyed the faces of his appointed commissioners. Highly intelligent and well-educated in the finer schools of Europe, Chihota had attained his stately position through shrewd maneuvering and his proven abilities at organization and management. Although serving under a Marxist leadership, Chihota himself had no desire to be considered a Communist, preferring the rewards of capitalism over the hardships of a socialist existence. He had expressed this blunt, but honest view to Tsonga Khama, the ruling prime minister of Zimbabwe, before accepting the internal affairs position. Impressed by Chihota's background and honesty, Khama conceded that if he were to take the position he would be granted certain high privileges.

Joshua Chihota now possessed one of the largest homes in the capital, owned three cars, and garnered a salary surpassed only by the prime minister and the president of Zimbabwe. Clearly, it was in Chihota's interest to see to it that there were no changes of leadership within the country, particularly a change that might involve General Moise Tobutu.

Chihota had tried every ploy available to him to discourage the leadership from inviting Tobutu to return for the elections, but to no avail. The matter had now taken on international implications and press coverage—none of which Chihota wanted, and for good reason. There had been trouble between Tobutu and Chihota from the outset of the guerrilla campaign to oust the white government of Rhodesia. Tobutu had considered Chihota no more than a coward who spouted revolutionary rhetoric but lacked the guts to take up a rifle to back up his own words. Chihota preferred to leave the bloody work to those he considered beneath his own station.

It was General Tobutu who learned of Chihota's personal bank accounts in Europe, accounts which grew steadily from money siphoned from donations to the guerrilla movement. Alerted to Tobutu's discovery, Chihota had barely made it out of the country, escaping only minutes before Tobutu's men arrived to take him into custody. Safe in Europe, Chihota denied all charges, of course, insisting that it was merely jealousy of his independent wealth and resentment for his education that had motivated Tobutu to make such ridiculous charges.

By the time hostilities had ceased, Tobutu was forced to flee the country, and the matter was all but forgotten. No, General Moise Tobutu was the last man on earth that Joshua Chihota wanted to see in any position of authority in Zimbabwe, not for two more years, anyway. That was how long he figured it would take him to obtain his goal of three million dollars in his Swiss bank accounts. After that, he didn't give a damn who ran Zimbabwe.

"Gentlemen," said Chihota, strolling to the windows overlooking the botanical gardens below, "for the past hour I have patiently listened to each of you. As of yet, I have not heard one word or mention of your dealings with the Tobutu factions that are planning for the general's return. Can you explain that, please?"

The men sitting around the table, handkerchiefs in hand, dabbed at their sweating faces, looking along the line at one another, each hoping that the other would answer the question they had so tactfully attempted to avoid.

"I am waiting, gentlemen," said Chihota, still standing at the windows, his back to the commissioners.

The darting eyes of the black men suddenly zeroed in on the commissioner of the Mashonaland West District. That, after all, was the birthplace of Moise Tobutu. The rumors of a secret organization forming in support of Tobutu had originated from that district, let him be the one to answer the minister's question.

Yielding to the pressures of his colleagues, the man from Mashonaland West cleared his throat and replied, "Mr. Minister, I am afraid that all of our attempts to locate and infiltrate this so-called secret organization have been unsuccessful. Frankly, sir, my men within the special branch have serious doubts that such an organization even exists. Our agents and informants have spent over a month investigating practically every village and town in the province and have yet to establish so much as one of these so-called Tobutu groups. If anything, Mr. Minister, I would say it is but a few individuals spreading rumors to stir up unrest among the people."

"Rumors, is it?" replied Chihota, turning away from the windows and circling slowly around the table. "What about the rest of you? Are you of the same opinion?"

Feeling renewed confidence now that one of their number had so eloquently expressed their own beliefs, the group nodded in agreement as each one mumbled, "Yes, only rumors!" "No, no such group exists." "Exaggerated, yes."

"Idiots!" Chihota suddenly screamed in a voice that silenced the room. The dabbing of faces became feverish now as frightened eyes sought to focus on anything to avoid looking at Chihota directly.

The minister went into a rage. His voice exploded within the room. "Do you honestly think that General Tobutu would risk returning to a country where his wife and two of his sons were killed, and his own life and that of his two remaining sons were threatened as well, if he did not believe he had sufficient support to obtain his goal? Idiots! I'm surrounded by total idiots! Each of you have a special branch of security personnel in your district, many of whom were trained and served under our white oppressors. The Rhodesians had no problem utilizing them efficiently in the past; I expect no less of you. Now, I will say this only once. You will locate and deal with this Tobutu situation before our next meeting, otherwise gentlemen, it will be your last. That I can promise you. Do I make myself clear?"

Silence hung heavily over the room. All eyes stared down at the table.

"I said, is that clear, goddamnit!" screamed Chihota at the top of his voice.

Again the heads about the table bobbed one by one in agreement among promises of results within days. Stepping to the door of the conference room, the minister flung it open.

"Now get the hell out of here and do your bloody jobs or I swear I'll have every last one of you working the chrome mines before the month is out! Go! Get out!"

There was a flurry of sliding chairs and a mad scramble for the exit. His anger still at its peak, Chihota slammed the door behind the last man to leave and stormed across the conference room into his own private office. Slumping into the plush leather

chair behind his desk, he leaned back and allowed his
rage to curtail itself slowly, all the time knowing that
his ranting and threats, even his anger, were wasted
on those morons who called themselves commissioners. He doubted there was enough intelligence among
the entire group to organize a blowjob in a whore-
house.

Rubbing his throbbing temples with his fingers,
Chihota's eyes focused on the calendar in front of
him. Three weeks and four days remained before the
elections. Tobutu would have to register as a candidate
before those four days were up; otherwise, he would
not be recognized on the ballot. He would have to
come soon.

Chihota began to rock slowly back and forth in his
chair. It was a steady movement that helped him think.
He began to weigh his options and measure the good
points against the bad. The simple solution was the
first to come to his mind—simply kill Tobutu the
minute he arrived at the airport. Hell, it had been
done before in other places. Look at the Philippines
and what happened to Aquino—gunned him down
right on the steps of the plane. It would be easy
enough to arrange. There was a special unit of the old
Rhodesian African Rifles who were fiercely loyal to
Chihota. They should be. After the war, they had been
no more than a ragtag army of ex-guerrilla fighters
with no home, no money, and nowhere to go. Chihota
transformed them into his own private elite guard and
supplemented their government pay with a monthly
bonus from his own private accounts. They would
willingly do whatever he asked of them, no questions
asked.

That thought was mentally chalked up on the "good" side. Almost immediately thereafter, the "bad point" of such an affair screamed for attention. Prime Minister Khama's open and highly publicized invitation for General Tobutu to return and participate in the first free and open elections of the country had garnered enormous praise from the United Nations and the world community. To gun the man down in the midst of a flood of reporters and cameramen would hardly be appropriate. The condemnation and economic effects would be horrendous. It would surely result in the loss of much-needed aid from a number of countries.

No, that simple option, as tantalizing as it was, was not the answer. All fingers of accusation would point directly to Khama, resulting in his dismissal as prime minister. No, Chihota had to be rid of Tobutu, but at the same time assure that Tsonga Khama remained in power. There could be no link between the government and the death of General Tobutu.

The chair came to a sudden stop. Chihota's eyes brightened as a crude sadistic smile broke at the corner of his mouth. "Of course," he whispered to himself, "and to think I called my commissioners idiots."

Shifting through the stacks of papers that littered his desk, he found the newspaper he was searching for. Midway down the front page along the left-hand column, there was a short three-paragraph story referring to the recent release of a former guerrilla leader and a brief mention that he had intentions of seeking political office. The man's name was Julius Keino—a name known throughout much of Zimbabwe, but hardly for his statesmanship. It was a name more associated with murder, terror, and torture. It was a wonder the press would take the man's boast of seeking political office seriously, let alone donate a sizable amount of space in their paper to a man that obviously had neither the backing nor the money to hope to obtain a political position within the government. It was laughable to say the least.

Chihota read the column three times before tossing the paper aside. A plan quickly began to form in his mind. Keino obviously hoped to edge his way into the parliamentary level of government, then, through his rather unique style of progression by elimination, move steadily up the ladder, possibly even to the presidential office.

Julius Keino was clearly a man of ambition—high ambition. A man who, if offered a chance to obtain a government position without having to go through the electoral process, would eagerly accept. Chihota was certain such a position could be made available in exchange for certain services rendered by a man of Keino's talents.

Drafting a carefully worded note for delivery to Julius Keino, Chihota called in his aide and ordered that the note be delivered within the hour. It was to be given to no one but Keino personally. As he leaned back in his chair, a multitude of plans began to form in Chihota's mind—plans that he and Julius Keino could discuss over a few drinks at the Chihota estate tonight. Of course those discussions would come after they had decided what position Keino would hold within the government of Zimbabwe.

CHAPTER FIVE

WISCO Corporation

Los Angeles, California

It was a little past eight in the evening when Stryker completed the interviews. Of the thirty-one names selected from the computer readouts, twenty-one people had met the requirements desired by the ex-Green Beret team leader. In this day and age of equal rights and equal opportunity, anyone would be hard-pressed to accuse Paul Stryker of discrimination. He was definitely an equal opportunity employer. One had only to go down the list of those selected to verify that.

Jean Pierre, a forty-eight-year-old Frenchman, was an ex-Legionnaire, gunrunner, and demolitions expert.

Nils Dalen was a Swede with a doctoral degree and a taste for the shadowy adventures of the mercenary world.

Meg Lathem, a hell-on-wheels black gal of twenty-eight, with a smile that could charm the socks off Bo

Jackson and a body that would make the Pope break his vows if he ever saw her naked, had an ex-military file that read like prerequisites for a school for Rambo: airborne school and helicopter flight school (where she finished first in her class), second place in the Boston Marathon, and no less than sixteen trophies for marksmanship while a member of the First Army Rifle Team. When informed by Stryker that if she was selected for the operation, there would be no special treatment afforded her because she was woman, her reply had been, "That's just fucking outstanding, Pops! Don't expect any—don't want any!"

Also included in the batch were Tsung Chen Lee, a former Red Chinese officer who had defected from China. When asked why he had defected, the answer was simple enough. "The pay sucked!" Lee was an expert in martial arts, as well as unique weapons such as the crossbow and the blowgun. This intrigued Stryker, himself a man that knew the value of silent weapons in the hands of an expert.

There was Charly Mangope, a former NCO with the Rhodesian SAS, or Special Air Service. He was a natural selection. His knowledge of the area and his Shona heritage were certain to endear him to Tobutu, who was also of Shona ancestry. If things went as planned, Mangope was certain to have a position in the general's reorganization of the military forces of Zimbabwe.

Jesse Fuller was an ex-Marine NCO with extensive background in operations and intelligence work, both in the military and out. He had served six years as a detective with the Atlanta Police Department. Among his chief duties while a member of Atlanta's finest was the personal security of VIPs moving in and out of the major metropolitan airport. His keen eye for suspicious people in large crowds and things out of the norm would be a major asset at Tobutu's political rallies.

Rounding out the final three that would constitute the primary team going in-country with Tobutu were John Young, Mike Renfro, and Joe Sampson, all ex-Green Berets and former members of the Delta Force. Willy McMillian was in Panama visiting one of his six ex-wives and would meet Stryker and the team in Harare in one week. The backup team consisted of eight men and two women, all Americans. They would remain on standby status in South Africa and be prepared to scramble should the primary team need assistance inside Zimbabwe.

All in all it had been a highly productive day's work. The final interview concluded, Stryker waited until the last applicant departed before he turned to Hayes and Richards, who sat on the couch across the room. They had monitored the selection process throughout the day.

"Well, gentlemen, looks like we're in business. Any questions?" asked Stryker.

Before either man could comment, the door opened and Randy York entered, balancing a tray of drinks precariously on one hand. Moving about the room, he offered each man a glass. Placing the tray aside, he lifted his drink in a toast, "To success, gentlemen."

Each man raised his glass in reply and sipped at their drink. Stryker noted a look of concern on the CIA director's face. Stepping back and seating himself on the edge of a desk, Stryker asked, "Is there a problem,

Mr. Hayes? You seem worried, sir."

All eyes were on the director as he answered, "Mr. Stryker, it appears your perception of expression is at its peak. As a matter of fact, there is something bothering me."

"Well, let's hear it, sir. I figure a man who is putting up three million dollars has every right to express his opinions whenever he wants," said Stryker with a grin.

Resting his drink on his knee, Hayes replied, "Far be it for me to tell you how to run this operation, but the selection of a woman for something as vital as protecting the life of a future leader of a country makes me a little nervous."

Stryker laughed, "My, my, who would have suspected the director of the CIA of being a chauvinist."

"Brother, you better not let Suzie hear that—she's a Gloria Steinem girl from way back," said York with a laugh.

"Now, wait a minute," cried Hayes, "I didn't mean it that way. What I meant was—well, hell, Stryker, how do you know she won't freeze up on you at a crucial moment if any shooting starts? I mean, it'll only take one shot to end this whole thing. Tobutu dies, and we're out of business."

Erin Richards joined in now, "Trust me, Rutherford, any woman who can say anything is 'fucking outstanding' about this operation, has no misconceptions of what is expected of her. I believe our girl Meg is at the top of the list in that category."

Hayes remembered the confidence in the young woman's voice when she made that statement to Stryker earlier in the day. It was true, the times they were a-changing, new attitudes, equal rights movements for everything from women to dogs to owls and even to trees. Hell, there were so many changes even the director of the CIA had a hard time keeping up with them.

"Oh, the hell with it," said Hayes, sliding back on the couch, "what am I worried about? Like they say, 'Hell hath no fury like a woman'—and all that shit! Cheers, gentlemen."

"Cheers!" came the reply from the others in the room.

Paul Stryker and his newly formed legion of professional bodyguards would depart in the morning for Puerto Rico and their first meeting with General Moise Tobutu.

Joshua Chihota's estate:

Outskirts of Harare Township

"So, as you can see, Mr. Keino—the elimination of General Tobutu would certainly be advantageous to both of us," said Chihota as he smiled and maneuvered the tongs over the man's glass to drop another ice cube in Keino's drink.

Keino did not reply nor did he return the smile. His cold, calculating black eyes watched Chihota's every move; his face was void of any expression. The minister could feel the stare of Keino's cold eyes on him. It was unnerving, so much so that Chihota dropped the ice tongs, and in a clumsy effort to catch them, knocked his own drink over.

"Damnit!" cried Chihota, purposely avoiding Keino's stare, "My word . . . this . . . this has just not been one of my better days."

Julius Keino remained silent, his eyes taking in
the flurry of activity as Chihota grabbed a bar towel
and began mopping up his mess. This was just the
type of Rhodesian black man that Julius Keino hated
with a passion—the educated ones, the ones who had
never really known poverty and what it meant to go
hungry month after month, men who never missed
an opportunity to show off their superior education
around fellow Africans, whom they considered far
below their station, with the use of words· such as,
"advantageous," or little phrases like, "My word" and
"just not my day." Keino still was not sure whether to
consider this man's offer or simply reach across the
bar and cut Chihota's throat from car to ear. For a
man of Keino's limited education, this was a difficult
decision. He found himself asking, Would this be—
"advantageous"!

The mess cleared away, Chihota began preparing
himself another drink. His hands were visibly shaking as he poured from the liquor bottle. It was plain
to Keino that the minister was more than a little
intimidated by his presence. It was also clear that
had Chihota been able to come up with another plan,
Keino would not be sitting in this fine home this
night. Joshua Chihota must truly be desperate. Could
he possibly be that afraid of Moise Tobutu? Or was
there something else? Nothing had been mentioned of
the minister's European bank accounts or the fact that
he had been stealing the country blind since its independence. There was no need for such discussions,
for Keino, as uneducated as he seemed, knew all
too well that power and high position bred greed and

thievery. It was the universal way of things. Even the Americans, with their holier-than-thou attitudes were not exempt from such corruption. One had only to look in the shadows of closed doors to realize the secretive deals and hidden bank accounts of their own senators and congressmen made them thieves, just as this snake Chihota was—highly educated thieves, but thieves, nonetheless.

Sipping his drink, Chihota finally looked up at Keino. "Well, my brother, what do you think? Would you be willing to consider a position within the government in exchange for your . . . your assistance with our problem?"

Convinced that Chihota had underestimated the intelligence of a streetwise African who had known nothing but hardship all his life, Keino shifted in his chair as he stared down at the melting ice cubes in his drink. Chihota must truly think him to be the fool. He needed no degree to realize that once Tobutu had been dealt with that he and his men would have to be eliminated by the government. They could not afford to leave anyone behind to tell the tale. Chihota, in his own crude and clumsy way, was setting him and his men up to take the fall for Tobutu's murder. Okay, so be it. Keino had a few plans of his own.

"I see no reason why we cannot work together, Chihota," said Keino softly, still staring into his glass. "In exchange, I want only one position in the government, that of assistant defense minister. Can that be arranged?"

"I . . . I suppose that could be arranged," replied Chihota.

Head still down, Keino's voice took on a more serious and threatening tone. "Mr. Chihota, should you have . . . let's say . . . a change of heart later on . . ." Keino's head suddenly shot up. With wide eyes, he stared directly into Chihota's eyes. "I shall personally gut you from your balls to your chest and stuff your intestines down your throat while you are dying."

Naked fear registered instantly in the minister's face, which suddenly changed to a sickly ashen gray as his mind formed a mental picture of such a horrid death. For the first time since entering the house Julius Keino smiled, and he broke out into a sadistic laugh. His words had had the desired effect.

"Come, Chihota, enjoy your drink." The terrorist smiled, "I am sure such things will not be necessary. If I cannot trust a brother African, then, who can I trust? Drink, my friend; then tell me why it is that your provincial governor of Mutula has failed to crush the nest of Tobutu supporters that are operating directly under his nose."

This statement brought another startled look from Chihota. "What are you talking about? Just this morning I met with my commissioners. Naknoa himself stated that there was no such activity in his area. The man does not possess the fortitude to lie to me. You must be mistaken, Keino," said Chihota with a renewed confidence that he was correct on this subject.

"Bullshit!" replied Keino. "Naknoa and his supposed force of elite incompetents have been stumbling all over these Tobutu instigators without recognizing them for what they are. One of my first duties as assistant defense minister will be to execute Naknoa and his whole damn bunch."

Refilling Keino's glass, Chihota asked, "How do you know all of this?"

Keino smiled for a second time that night as he replied, "I, and a few of my men, ask the right questions of the right people, in the right way, Mr. Chihota. We have very persuasive methods I can assure you. Eventually our questions led us to Mutula Province. There we discovered fifty Tobutu supporters in this particular group. They operate much the same as we did when we were fighting the whites for independence. They split up portions of their printing press and the materials. They hid them in their homes. Every Friday, they gather at a different cattle farm or house, reassemble the press, and run off Tobutu's literature, pamphlets, and posters."

"Friday!" said Chihota with excitement, "Why . . . why that's today. This is Friday night! Where are they right now? Do you know the meeting place? I can phone Naknoa—they can surround the . . ."

"No! You will call no one," said Keino forcefully. "Do not forget, I have seen firsthand the ignorance of your Naknoa and his forces. No, tonight, my men and I will handle the situation." Keino paused and cast his eyes on Chihota again. "Your major concern will be how to explain to the press the news of the massacre that is about to take place."

Chihota's color began to fade once more. "My God, you mean to kill all of them?" he asked.

"Every last one," answered Keino before downing his drink and slamming his glass down onto the bar. "Now if you will excuse me, Mr. Minister, I would not want to miss the fun. Remember our deal, Chihota. I for one am a man of my word. What I say—I do. Sleep well, my brother."

Keino's demonic laughter followed him out the door. With his hands trembling, Chihota moved from behind the bar and eased himself up on a bar stool. "My Lord, what have I done? The man is a homicidal maniac—even worse, a maniac with ambition—very high ambitions at that."

Grabbing the bottle of whiskey, he refilled his glass, raised it to his lips, and gulped the liquor down in one long swallow. It didn't help. No amount of alcohol was going to take away the feeling that he, Joshua Chihota, had just made a deal with the son of the devil—if not the devil himself.

Puerto Rico

Tobutu's Safe House

Upon their arrival, Stryker and the team were met by a CIA agent and members of the WISCO staff. They would secure the aircraft and remain on guard around it during the night while the team dined with General Tobutu and got some sleep. Transportation was on hand in the form of brightly colored minibuses. There was a sense of excitement among the team members as they boarded the buses for the trip to the CIA-owned estate where General Tobutu was staying. Of the group, Paul Stryker was the only one who had ever met the flamboyant ex-guerrilla leader. He knew his team was in for a treat.

Moise Tobutu was standing on the front steps as the buses began to arrive. Decked out in his full-dress uniform with its regalia of brightly colored ribbons and metals of silver, gold, and bronze, he was an impressive sight indeed. The general appeared to have put on a little weight, but he was obviously in excellent condition for a man of fifty-nine. Sprinkles of gray were visible along the sides of his thick black hair. His face was full and round, not quite black, but rather a dark bronze.

Seeing Stryker move down the steps of the first bus, the general broke into a wide smile, displaying large, shining white teeth so perfect that they would make a Hollywood actress moan with envy. Moving down the steps of the house, Tobutu reached out his hand to greet his one-time adversary.

"Ah, Sergeant Paul Stryker—it is good to see an old enemy looking so well," said Tobutu.

Remembering the general's love of military tradition, Stryker stiffened, clicked his heels together, and snapped off a smart salute in perfect form. His action received a similar response from Tobutu.

"You appear very fit, General," said Stryker with a smile.

Formalities over, Tobutu grasped Stryker's hand and pumped it tightly as he said, "The moment they told me who they were sending, I knew I would be in competent hands. Come . . . come inside. Bring your people. I want to meet them all."

Stryker waved the group inside. They followed the general through the well-decorated estate and out onto the patio where Tobutu called the servants to bring on the drinks. Across the way, a huge pig was being roasted on a spit. Long tables covered in white silk tablecloths held bowls of brightly colored salads and fruits. Silver trays were piled high with broiled shrimp,

fried shrimp, and shrimp cocktails prepared in larger-
than-normal crystal goblets of finely cut glass and filled
with blood-red sauce. Other trays were piled high with
ham, chicken, roast beef, and turkey. Surveying the
scene, Stryker grinned as he said, "I see you're still
having to rough it, huh, General."

Tobutu laughed a husky, friendly laugh, as he
replied, "You Americans have a knack for knowing
a man's weaknesses, Sergeant Stryker. I am afraid
the long periods between meals during the war in
Rhodesia have made me more appreciative of the
wonders of excellent food in unlimited supply." Patting
his stomach, he winked, as he said, "As you can see,
your government has exploited that weakness."

Stryker nodded in agreement. He knew the feeling
all too well. More than once, in Vietnam he would
have gladly traded everything he had for one Big
Mac with fries or a pizza. Turning to the team,
Tobutu spread his arms wide and proclaimed loudly,
"Please feel free to indulge yourselves, my friends.
What you see before you has been prepared in your
honor."

The general did not have to issue the invitation
again. There was a clattering of plates and silverware
as the team swarmed over the feast that lay before
them. Stryker and the general had just picked up their
plates when they were joined by Bryon Tolbridge, the
CIA case officer responsible for the general's safety
while he was in Puerto Rico. A personable man in
his mid-fifties, Tolbridge took the two men aside and
suggested they join him in the communications facility
at the rear of the estate. There was a classified report
coming in from an operative in Zimbabwe. Setting his

plate aside, Stryker joined them and walked around the house to the ComCenter.

"Message is just coming in now, sir," said the young radio operator as they entered the room.

Tolbridge waited until the printer signaled the message was completed. Then he tore the hard copy of the deciphered message free. Scanning it quickly, he shook his head. Passing the message to the general, Tolbridge said, "I'm sorry, General, I'm afraid that puts to rest any hopes that we might have had that Prime Minister Khama would conduct an honest and fair election."

The message was from a CIA operative, code-named Sidney, inside Zimbabwe. It described in detail the attack on the fifty members of the Tobutu group in Mutula. There had been no survivors. The lucky ones were shot fleeing the ranch house that had been set ablaze while they were inside. Those less fortunate were shoved or thrown back into the inferno and burned alive. The minister of internal affairs planned to hold a news conference and blame the massacre on a tribal feud. The statement would be carefully worded so as not to refer to any particular political group, especially Tobutu supporters.

The joyfulness of earlier today was forgotten now, as Tobutu sadly uttered, "Already it begins. Fifty people dead, and I have not even set foot in my homeland. I cannot help but wonder if my poor people will ever know peace in their lifetime."

Stryker, knowing that his words would seem inadequate, but seeing the disillusionment in the general's face, placed his hand on the big man's shoulder and said, "Only when they have a man they can trust and respect to lead them, will they know such freedom. You, General, are that man."

Tobutu's eyes returned to the paper in his hands, "I wonder, Mr. Stryker, if these fifty would agree with you now?"

"Of course they would General. Don't forget, I have seen firsthand your ability to lead. Your people have not forgotten you. The death of these fifty can only serve to draw hundreds more to your cause. You know I am right, don't you?" said Stryker.

Passing the paper back to Tolbridge, Tobutu placed his hand over Stryker's. "Thank you my friend. Please ask my guests to forgive my poor manners. I will talk with them tomorrow. But for now, I would like to spend some time alone. There are many things that weigh heavy upon my mind." Turning to the CIA man, he continued, "Mr. Tolbridge, would it be permissible for me to go for a walk along the beach? It is very pleasant there."

"Of course, sir," replied Tolbridge, "but I'm afraid two of my men will have to go along with you."

Tobutu sighed deeply as he answered, "I understand. Perhaps one day, even I will know the freedom of a simple walk without fear for my life. Thank you, Mr. Tolbridge."

As the general went out the door, Tolbridge signaled two of his agents standing near the door to follow. The two followed Tobutu into the darkness, remaining a respectable but security-minded distance to the rear.

"Damn shame," said Tolbridge, passing the message back to the operator for his files. "I've really gotten to know that ol' boy pretty well since we've been here, and I'll tell you something, Stryker. I've spent over half my life working these damn African assignments and I've seen 'em come and go, but this guy is by far the best prospect for peace in that region that I've seen come along in twenty years. I understand Tobutu saved your ass once. That right?"

"Sure did," said Paul. "I owe him."

"Well, judging by that mess at Mutula, you're going to get your chance to return the favor. You know they'll be after the old man as soon as you get settled in, don't you?"

"No illusions here, Mr. Tolbridge," relied Paul. "Knew that when I took the job—so did all my people I brought with me. Any idea who might have been behind the cremation at Mutula?"

Tolbridge hesitated for a moment, considering whether or not to answer the question.

"Come on, Tolbridge, this is no time to be holding back on me," said Stryker. "This damn thing's going to be hard enough as it is. You know who orchestrated this little massacre, don't you?"

"Yes, we do," replied Tolbridge. "Sidney was one of the original organizers of the Tobutu support group and was on site when it went down, but just happened to be fortunate enough to have been outside when the attack began."

"Who was it?" asked Stryker.

"Keino—Julius Keino and about thirty of his cut-throats."

"I figured as much," sighed Stryker. "So who is this Sidney?"

A frown rippled across the elderly agent's brow. "No fucking way, Stryker. It has taken us two years to get Sidney set up in there, and nobody is going to walk in and blow that cover, not even for Tobutu. Now, you got one answer you wanted. One out of two ain't bad."

"Fair enough, Tolbridge. What I know can't hurt me, right? Come on, let's join the others." Turning to the door, Stryker paused, then said, "Oh yeah, if you don't mind, I'd rather we didn't say anything about this until the morning. I want my people to enjoy themselves tonight and get a good night's sleep. It may be the last chance they'll have for a while."

"Whatever you say, Paul. It's your show, your team, and your responsibility," said Tolbridge.

Yeah, thought Stryker as they walked outside. How many times had he heard those very same words? The words never seemed to change, just the places and the faces of those who would do the dying.

Tolbridge woke Stryker at first light. The team leader wanted to get an early start. Going from room to room, Stryker began rousing the team from the last peaceful sleep they would know until after the operation. Entering the last room, Paul yelled, "Okay, girls, hit the deck! It's game time. Let's move it Young— come on Renfro, let's go."

Turning to the bed in the corner, Stryker grabbed a pillow and tossed it at Joe "the Moose" Sampson, hitting the 260-pound giant squarely in the face. The big man didn't bat an eye. Swatting at his nose as if the pillow had been nothing more than an oversized mosquito, Big Joe rolled over and continued to snore, still sound asleep.

"Jesus! One of you guys toss a grenade over there

and see if you can wake Moose up, okay? We're out of here in an hour."

"You got it, boss," said Johnny Young, picking up one of his boots and going toward the bathroom to fill it with ice cold water, "We'll be ready."

Stepping out into the hallway, Stryker saw Nils Dalen, wearing only a pair of bright red, tight-fitting boxer shorts. He was standing in the doorway of the large bathroom at the end of the hall. Meg Latham, wearing nothing but bra and panties, was trying to get past him to take a shower, but the smiling Swede, openly admiring her curvaceous body, refused to let her pass. Shifting her weight to her right foot, Meg flashed Nils a sexy smile as she asked, "Tell me, Dr. Dalen, have you ever seen . . ."

"Nils . . . please call me Nils. Dr. Dalen is so formal under the circumstances, don't you think?" said the handsome Swede, puffing out his well-formed bare chest covered in a mass of golden hair.

"If you like," replied Meg. "So tell me, Nils, being a doctor and all, have you ever encountered the flutter organism syndrome?"

Stryker, overhearing the question, leaned back against the wall and folded his arms across his chest. He was just as interested as the confused doctor in hearing more about this unheard-of medical term.

"Well, have you, Doctor?" asked Meg.

"Uh . . . no, I can't say I have. This must be a new ailment that I am not aware of. Just what are the symptoms of this thing?"

Meg, her smile still fixed, said, "Coarse hair protruding from the eyeballs, usually preceded by acute pain."

"My word, that sounds terrible. Are there many cases of this new syndrome?" asked Nils with professional concern.

Straightening herself up, Meg separated her feet slightly and squared her shoulders with the door as she calmly answered, "You fuckin' A right there are. Three cases I know of for sure. All three were assholes that wanted to fuck with me before I had my morning coffee. I drop-kicked their balls up to their eyesockets—it was one of those pain/pleasure things, you know. Hurt like hell, but they got horny every fuckin' time they blinked. Now, you want to get the hell out of my way or stay horny all day, Doc?"

The Swede's mouth was still hanging open as Stryker laughingly said, "I think if I were you, Nils, I'd move. Who wants to spend all morning trimming their eyeballs?"

Nils quickly stepped out of the way. Looking back over her shoulder at Paul, and still grinning, Meg winked at him, then, went into the bathroom and closed the door. Moving down the hall past Stryker, Nils shook his head as he whispered, "Jes! That gal's as hard as a dinosaur's toenails! You better make sure we've got plenty of coffee around for this trip."

Chen Lee and Jean Pierre came out of their room. They were already dressed and ready to go down for breakfast. Stryker joined them. General Tobutu was already at the table, a pile of sausage, and ham beside the scrambled eggs. The dress uniform was gone, replaced by camouflage fatigues. A red beret bearing the crest of the Rhodesian airborne was cigarette-rolled and tucked under the left epaulet of the fatigue shirt. The general was his usual jubilant self again. The walk on the beach last night had helped. Looking up from his plate, he waved the others to chairs as he said, "Ah, gentlemen, you are the first arrivals. Please be seated. The breakfast is outstanding."

No sooner were the three seated than a host of servants appeared, took their plates, and moved to the buffet. Selecting portions of each main item, they filled the plates for the guests and returned them to the surprised soldiers of fortune. Lee and Pierre watched the procedure, looking at one another, while at the same time saying, "Owwwwh—high society at last."

The four men at the table were still laughing as Tolbridge entered the room. Seating himself, he said, "Good to see everyone in top-notch spirits this morning."

They bid him good morning as the remainder of the team began to arrive. Meg was the last to enter the room. Stryker and the others started to stand as she approached her seat. Pointing straight at Stryker, she shook her head from side to side as she said, "Don't even think about it. No special treatment, remember. I'm just one of the boys."

Stryker nodded politely and remained seated, as did the others. Nils leaned forward slightly, looking around the barrel chest of Joe Sampson. Smiling at Meg, he fluttered his eyelids wildly at the black beauty. A grin started at the corner of her lips as she looked away, trying hard not to break out into laughter. The fact that he had shown an interest in her had touched that spot of femininity that she tried so often to keep hidden. She had to admit, Nils was one hell of a good-looking guy.

Jesse Fuller and Charly Mangope, sitting next to each other, stared across the table, watching Doc's rather strange flurry of eyelid maneuvers. "Look there, Charly," said Fuller, "out of the States only twenty-four hours and Doc's already lost it. This ought to be a real fun experience 'fore it's over."

"Without a doubt," replied the African.

Breakfast over, Stryker waited until everyone's coffee cups were refilled. Then he stood.

"Okay, folks, I guess it's time we go over the game plan before we take the field. We all know why we're here. I wish I could say this was going to be an easy one, but I'm afraid the opposition has already demonstrated their intentions." Stryker went on to describe in detail the massacre at Mutula. "Within twelve hours, we will be landing in Harare, the capital of Zimbabwe. As you know the elections are still three weeks away. That's a long time, and time has a way of breeding complacency. I'm sure you all would agree. Therefore, it is imperative that we stay sharp and on our toes at all times. Our objective is to see that General Tobutu has a fair and equal opportunity to participate in these elections without getting his head blown off. I don't feel the opposition will try anything at the airport—too many press people will be there to greet us. However, we'll play it tight anyway. One thing I can promise you—the closer it gets to the actual election day, the more determined they're going to be to take the general out of the game. We have to be ready. The advantage is theirs. They can hit us anytime, anyplace. Each of you were chosen for this job because of your experience, powers of observation, and your shooting skill. When it comes, and it will come, believe me, we must make every effort to avoid trapping the civilians in a cross fire. But, if it comes down to a choice between your own life or that of the general, remember, your mission is to guarantee the safety of General Tobutu—at any cost. Is that understood?"

It was a somber-faced, serious group that nodded their understanding of their leader's meaning.

"Good," said Paul as he continued, "you will notice that we are making this trip without the normal assortment of automatic weapons, grenades, and shotguns that would seem warranted in this type of situation. The reason for that is Prime Minister Khama. His policy is that only the army and his special police are authorized to carry such weapons in the country, or so they have informed us. That situation will be remedied within hours of our arrival, compliments of our friend, Francois Dibó, with whom many of you have had dealings before. Until then, we will have to rely on the Berettas. I do not see that as a problem. Your abilities with a handgun is another of the reasons you are here."

Joe Sampson shook his head as he said, "Yeah, you're right Paul, but you've been in Africa before. You know how these boys work. If they can't get to you with a few hit men, they'll come at us with a mob. Now, I know we're all pretty good at this shit, but with only eleven folks following the general all over the countryside, we could find our asses in a tight box in a hurry. An' I doubt ol' Khama would be in any hurry to provide us with a hell of a lot of support. Know what I mean?"

"You're right there, Moose. That's why we'll have Randy York with another team on standby just across the border in South Africa. Mr. Hayes and Mr. Richards have managed to acquire a small contingent of assault helicopters and UH1H Hueys to serve as a kind of mini-air force. If this thing starts going to shit on us, they'll come in like the cavalry to pull our butts out of the fire."

The answer brought a look of relief from some of those in the room. "Well, that's it. Any questions?" asked Stryker.

There were none. Turning to Tobutu, he asked, "Would you like to say a few words, General?"

Tobutu stood at the end of the table. His voice cracked with emotion as he said, "Ms. Lathem and gentlemen—mere words cannot express my gratitude, nor that of my people, for what you are doing. Hopefully, soon, you will receive the full honors you deserve for the risks that you are about to undertake. May God bless and protect us all. Thank you."

The entire table of volunteers rose as one and saluted the general and future prime minister of Zimbabwe.

Prime Minister's Office

Harare, Zimbabwe

Tsonga Khama was in a rage. His high-pitched voice resounded off the walls as he flailed his arms about like a wild man, screaming, "You must be insane, Chihota! How dare you take it upon yourself to assume that I would ever go along with such a plan. Julius Keino, for Christ's sake! You ally me with a known terrorist—a butcher of all things. And on top of that, the man is a mental maniac. Assistant defense minister? You must be insane yourself."

Chihota remained calm as he sat in a chair next to the minister's desk. "But, sir, as I have attempted to explain to you, that was only a position promised, and only after General Tobutu was eliminated. Should Mr. Keino be killed immediately after the act, I believe that would alleviate the necessity for this conversation, do you not agree?"

Khama, his arm waving at an end, returned to his desk.

"You are playing a dangerous game, Chihota. Julius Keino is not the fool he would have people think. He is a very dangerous man. You may yet find yourself wishing you had not involved yourself with such a man."

With his usual air of cool confidence, Chihota replied, "Keino does not bother me. I have sufficient forces at my disposal to deal with him. It is Tobutu that is the real problem. The reports of his growing support are true, my friend. If I were you, that would be my primary worry."

Wrinkles of concern etched their way across Khama's face as he asked, "You have confirmed this yourself?"

"Yes, we have."

"The fifty killed in Mutula—were they Tobutu's people?"

"Yes, they were. Mr. Keino handled that little problem for us himself, last night. Free of charge, I might add."

Chihota watched a small bead of sweat race down the side of the minister's face as Khama said, "Yes, of course, from the reports I have read of the massacre, I should have recognized the man's work." Pausing,

Khama lit a cigarette before asking, "Okay, Joshua, now that you have made us part of a massacre, what is your next plan of action? I hope neither of you have illusions of assassinating Tobutu at the airport. That would certainly spell disaster for all of us."

Amazing thought, Chihota. At times, Khama could actually seem a man of intelligence, rather than the weak-kneed, bumbling fool that he actually was—a fool whom Chihota had learned to play like the keys of a broken-down piano.

"No, Tsonga; however, I must admit, the idea did come to mind briefly. But, of course, you are correct. There will be too many press people there. They almost expect an attempt on the general's life. I think it best that we allow Tobutu to arrive safely, give his meaningless interviews, and go virtually undisturbed about his business for a week or so. The press is so fickle that they will gradually lose interest and go on to other things. That is when we will strike. I thought I might write you a fitting speech welcoming Tobutu back home. It could be broadcast over television and radio tonight. Then when he is killed, I shall write another in which you will express deep regret for a fallen hero and worthy opponent."

The worry lines began to fade from Khama's chubby little face. He appeared more at ease with himself, now. His loyal aide, Chihota, had taken this problem head-on and was being his usual proficient self. "Yes, a eulogy, I like that. Fine, Chihota, I leave this entire matter in your hands. I know you will not fail me."

Chihota stood, "Thank you for your confidence, Prime Minister. Now, if you will excuse me, I have work to do."

"But of course, you are excused," said Khama with a hint of superior authority that turned Chihota's stomach.

Walking to the door, Chihota paused, looked back over his shoulder at Khama, and said, "Oh, yes, there is one other matter, sir."

"Yes, what is it now, Chihota?"

"Keino wants to kill the commissioner responsible for Mutula."

"What? Naknoa! But . . . but, he is my wife's brother!"

"Yes, I know; however, he was also the one responsible for allowing the Tobutu organization to be created under his very nose. If it had not been for Keino, that very group would have caused a great deal of harm during the election."

The room was silent. Khama's case of nerves suddenly returned. Wringing his hands, the man tried desperately to seek a solution to this new dilemma, but lacked the capabilities or intestinal fortitude to overrule the reply that Chihota obviously wanted to hear.

Chihota was enjoying this. "I must have an answer, sir. I am to meet with Keino within the hour. He will want to know your answer."

His hands stopped. Clutching them tightly together, Khama closed his eyes. Unable to say the words, he nodded his approval.

"Fine. It will be done," said Chihota as he left the office, closing the door quietly behind him. Khama moaned softly and lowered his head to his clenched hands. The knowledge of one's own weakness can often be a painful thing.

Passing by his office, Chihota informed his staff

that he would not be back for the remainder of the
day. He could be reached at his home if he was
needed. Pleased with himself, Chihota whistled as he
unlocked the door of his car, climbed inside, flipped
on the air-conditioning, then wheeled out into the
busy midmorning traffic of the city. He had handled
Khama with ease. The fool—excusing him, Chihota,
as if he were some common servant. It had taken all
his strength not to laugh in the oversized clown's face.
But, then, that had not been necessary. The request to
do away with Naknoa had had a much better effect. Of
course, Julius Keino was going to be surprised. He had
made no such request. It was only Chihota's hurt pride
that had made him single out Naknoa, knowing full
well of the relationship between the two men. Watching Khama's expressions of tormented weakness had
given him much more satisfaction than simply laughing in the man's face.

Pulling into the circular drive of his estate, Chihota
entered the house to find Keino and three of his men
standing at the bar. Bantu, the elderly head servant,
rushed up to his employer. "I am sorry, sir, they
simply forced their way in. They said you . . . you
were expecting them, sir. Should I call the police?"

"No, Bantu, that is all right. I will handle it. You
and the others may go for the day, with full pay, of
course. Now, go tell the others."

"Yes, sir. Thank you, sir."

Waiting until the old man had departed, Chihota
walked to the bar. Keino's eyes were watery and
bloodshot. The man was on the verge of being drunk,
as were the other three. Two bottles of his best whiskey
lay empty on the bar. Reaching for a third, Chihota

fixed himself a drink as he said, "Celebrating a little early, are we?"

The three men beside Keino paused from their drinking and fixed their hard-looking eyes upon Chihota. One slammed his glass on the bar, pulled a knife from the back of his belt, and slowly turned it in his hand. A look of blood was in his eyes.

"Back off, you ignorant kaffir!" said Keino, "This is our employer. He's the money. Now, put that thing away and behave yourself."

Gradually, the knife was lowered, and it disappeared back into the man's belt.

"Not wise to irritate my men, Chihota. They do not have the tolerance for an educated kaffir that I have," said Keino.

Chihota cringed, he hated that word—"kaffir." It was a name derived from an Arabic word meaning "infidel" or "heathen." Here it was the same as a white man calling a black a "nigger" in America.

"So tell me, my new partner, what did your prime minister think of our dealings in Mutula last night? Was he pleased?" asked Keino.

Taking a drink before he answered, Chihota said, "Not at first. I found it necessary to tell him of our alliance and of your new position in the government following Tobutu's demise."

"And?"

"He was very appreciative of your services. As a matter of fact, he personally requested that you administer the same service upon the commissioner of Mutula for his incompetence. Can that be arranged?"

Keino seemed shocked by the statement. He, too, was aware that the commissioner was Khama's brother-in-law. "But, of course, it will be my pleasure. You know, maybe this Khama and I have more in common than I thought."

Another of Keino's men entered the house. Rushing up to his boss's side and eyeing Chihota suspiciously, he leaned forward and whispered something in Keino's ear. Chihota could not hear what was said, but he saw Keino's eyes widen. A smile crossed his face. "What is it?" asked Chihota.

"Good news, my friend. My sources report that General Tobutu is airborne at this very moment and will arrive at the Harare Airport at three this afternoon. By three-fifteen, I will be the new assistant defense minister."

"No!" cried Chihota, louder than he had intended. His action again drew a host of hard looks from the men at the bar. "I . . . I mean, no—we can't do that, Keino. The press will be there. We cannot afford such an incident in their presence."

"Why not?" laughed Keino. "It would make great television. People hate to admit it, but they love to watch violence in all its raw, unadulterated form, the bloodier, the better."

"Perhaps," agreed Chihota, nervously, "but not General Tobutu, not now. All you have to do is keep an eye on him for the rest of the week. I want no attempts on his life until I say so. Is that clear? I will tell you when."

Keino stopped laughing. The half-drunken smile fell from his face. His eyes darkened, taking on a hateful look as he stared at Chihota. "You do not order me about like one of your kaffir servants! Do you hear me, Chihota? I am not the spineless jellyfish that Khama is. I do as I please, when I please. No man, white or black, will ever tell me what I must do. No! Never again."

Reaching out suddenly, Keino twisted his fist into the collar of Chihota's shirt and slowly drew the man's face to within inches of his own. "Now, do you understand what I am saying, you overeducated kaffir?"

Keino's men were watching intently with smiles on their faces. The choking grip of Keino's was so tight that Chihota's face was turning a beet red, and he could hardly breathe. Blinking that he understood, he had tried to nod but found he couldn't move.

"That's a good boy," taunted Keino, as he pushed Chihota away from him. "Now, I, Keino, will tell you what will be done, not some paper-shuffling college boy who knows nothing of killings." Keino paused a second and rubbed at the stubble on his chin. "Perhaps you are right about the airport, but we will not wait a week either. We will allow Tobutu a few days to organize a schedule; then, we will pick our place and time and kill him."

The color was beginning to return to Chihota's face as he massaged the back of his neck. The fact that he had at least convinced Keino to forego an airport attack was some consolation for the pain he had just endured. Watching Keino's mouth move as he spouted tales of of his past battles with the Rhodesians, Chihota was not hearing a word he was saying, but rather envisioning that same mouth pleading for mercy as his African Rifles tied the maniac to a pole before an execution squad. Chihota, a man who normally went out of his way to avoid violence, would personally give the commands on that day and love every minute of it.

The thought forced a smile which Keino mistook for one of satisfaction with his authority.

"Ah, that is better, my brother. There is no need for such hostilities between allies. Did I hurt you, brother? I am sorry if I did."

"No, I am fine," replied Chihota picking up his drink.

"That is good. Yes, good." Finishing his whiskey, Kcino set his glass down. Waving the others out, he said, "Come, we have work in Mutula."

Keino's followers were not as ignorant of their leader's sudden rages as had been Chihota. Setting their half-filled glasses down quickly, they turned and left immediately. "Later, Chihota," said Keino, "next when I come, I shall set a time to be rid of Moise Tobutu."

Turning on his heels and walking toward the door, Keino broke into his usual sadistic laughter. Without looking back, he said, "I will give Naknoa your regards before we drench him in gasoline and set him on fire. Sleep well, my brother."

Thankful for the silence of his own house, Chihota began to formulate a plan for the execution of Julius Keino. The press would be invited to witness the death of the man who killed one of Zimbabwe's greatest heroes in the struggle for equality. Naturally, since it was to be a public execution, they would have to cut the insolent fool's tongue out first; they wouldn't want him screaming the details of his dealings with the government. Chihota had planned to have Keino and his men gunned down after they killed Tobutu, but the choking incident had changed all that. "We shall see who is the kaffir in the end, Keino," he whispered as he poured himself a drink and sat down at the bar. It was perfect. Seeing his image in the mirror behind the bar, he lifted his glass and toasted himself. "To the master of perfection."

CHAPTER SIX

The chartered aircraft procured by Randy York had been modified at the midsection to provide for a small but sufficient operations area. A detailed full-color map of Zimbabwe lay spread across a plotting board. Stryker and Tobutu were working on a proposed schedule for their first week of activities, selecting various townships in which to begin the general's campaign. Stryker suggested they bypass the smaller, more distant villages and concentrate their efforts on the larger towns and cities. Tobutu reluctantly agreed. The general wanted to visit them all, but time limitations would not permit them the luxury.

As Tobutu circled specific locations, Stryker studied the terrain markings for the area. Those which appeared to present a high probability for ambush were plotted and the coordinates recorded. Upon arrival in Harare, Stryker planned to have Young and Renfro set up their satellite as soon as they reached the house the embassy had leased for Tobutu and his bodyguards. Utilizing WISCO's sat time, Young would make the uplink with the satellite, transmit the coordinates directly to WISCO's headquarters, and request that Richards arrange for high-intensity photos of the coordinated areas. Once acquired, the pictures would be transmitted back to the team via secure fax to the American Embassy in Harare. An intelligence folder would be established for each proposed area and reviewed before each day's travel into that area.

Meg Latham stepped through the curtains that separated the small operations room from the rest of the aircraft. Tobutu looked up and smiled at her as she entered.

"Excuse me, Paul, the pilot wanted me to let you know that we will begin our descent into Harare in ten minutes."

"Thanks, Meg. On your way back up front, let Young and Renfro know I'll have some work for them when we get settled in."

"Will do," she replied, disappearing through the curtains.

Turning to Tobutu, Paul said, "We better get this stuff gathered up. We can continue our work at the house."

Tobutu was still smiling his easygoing smile. "I'm certainly impressed by your optimism, Paul. How do you know we will even reach the house?"

Stryker grinned. "Because the only way you won't get there is if I'm dead, and I don't plan on checking out of the game that early. Besides, unless I miss my guess, the only shooting at the airport will be from flashbulbs and television cameras. Even Khama isn't stupid enough to try a hit with the world watching on live television."

"Live," said Tobutu with a surprised look.

"You got it, General. CNN will be there—that means the world will be watching. If you doubt that, just ask Saddam Hussein how good their coverage is, and how it can affect public opinion."

"No need, my friend. I saw what happened to that fool. However, it is pleasing to know that my sons will have the opportunity to see that I have arrived safely."

Folding away the maps and charts, the two men joined the others and settled in for the landing at Harare. Stryker could only imagine the feelings that must be flowing through Tobutu at this moment. He had been gone from his homeland so long. They were feelings that Stryker himself had experienced each time he had returned from tours in Vietnam. Now that he thought of it, this was quite similar: overjoyed at being home, but knowing that there were also those who hated and despised you.

The plane touched down with a gentle bump and was guided to an area designated for the arrival of VIPs. Looking out the side window, Stryker saw the mob of press people he had expected. He pointed them out to the general, who nodded as he said, "As usual, you are correct, my friend. Let us hope that the remainder of your prediction will be as accurate."

Stryker winked. "You got it, General. Sir, I'd like you to remain on the aircraft until I have had a chance to disperse my people."

Tobutu nodded again, fully understanding the reasons for the request. Optimism and predictions were nice, but a man did not risk his life on such things. Stryker's team was on its feet as the plane rolled slowly to a stop. Standing near the door, Paul said, "Okay, gang, it's game time. Meg, you, Lee, and Pierre head for the roof of the building behind the press corps. It looks like the army has placed some troops up there for security. You guys get up there and keep 'em honest. Moose, you and Mangope flank the press and keep moving around. Nils, you and I will stay with the general. We'll keep him between us. Fuller, you and Renfro handle the off-loading of our stuff from the plane to the embassy vans; then set me up a corridor between the fence and the plane. Any questions?" There were none.

"Okay, then, I guess we're ready. Just remember, if you have to shoot, make sure of your targets and then take them down hard. Let's go to work," said Stryker.

As their boss cracked the seal on the door, the team members checked their weapons, switched them off safe, and slid the weapons into the back of their belts, flipping their long-tailed safari jackets back to conceal the flat black weapons.

Stryker swung the door open and motioned Meg forward as the off-loading ramp was being slid into place. "Go," commanded Stryker.

The three destined for the roof raced down the steps, moving swiftly past the crowd of reporters and into the building. Moose Sampson and Mangope took up positions around the press, moving slowly back and forth on the flanks of the crowd. Waving for Nils to bring the general forward, Stryker kept his eyes fixed on the rooftop. Meg and the others suddenly appeared among Khama's soldiers. She spoke to one of the men, then pointed to the plane, as Pierre and Lee, moving casually, positioned themselves between the soldiers and the plane.

Tobutu and Nils were at the door. Stryker held out his hand, motioning for the general to wait. Two other soldiers now joined the first, who was speaking with Meg. Below, the press was becoming impatient. They began pushing their way toward the plane. Apparently satisfied with Meg's explanation of why they were on the roof, the soldiers went back to their positions. Meg signaled the all clear to Stryker.

"Okay, General, you're home. From here on out, it's your show," said Paul. "I'll go down first, then, you, then, Nils. I'd appreciate it, sir, if you'd make this kind of short. We can call a press conference at the house later where we have better control over the security."

"I understand. I agree that would be best. Shall we go?"

Stryker stepped out onto the ramp and scanned the area. Three hundred yards to the right of the building and beyond the fence stood hundreds of Africans with banners welcoming Tobutu home. A solid line of Khama's security police stood between them and the fence. Halfway down the steps, Stryker could feel eyes watching him, not just the press. Rather, a sixth sense told him he was under the scrutiny of one particular person. Reaching the bottom of the steps, Stryker moved to the side, his gaze darted around the crowd. Then he saw him, a big African with a camera and a telephoto lens, standing near a hangar door two hundred yards to the left—Khama's secret police, no doubt. It was certain he had taken pictures of everyone getting off the plane. By sundown the faces of every member of the team would be distributed to the police and the army.

Waving to crowds at the fence, Tobutu moved to the podium and microphones in front of the press. True to his word, but disappointing the press people who had spent over an hour standing in the heat, the general kept his remarks short. He was glad to be home again and had high hopes for his country. Announcing that a press conference would be called later, he abruptly ended his speech by saying he would answer questions at that time. This brought a moan from the reporters, who continued to bombard him with questions anyway. Tobutu looked to Stryker for direction.

The gear secured, Renfro waved to indicate that they were ready to go. Flanking the general, Stryker and Nils began moving him toward the vehicles parked twenty yards away.

"Uh oh, bureaucrats," said Nils, nodding toward the vans. Stryker saw the two well-dressed men approaching them. One was in his late fifties, the other in his early forties: embassy brass.

"Damnit," muttered Stryker. "Sons-of-bitches couldn't resist a chance to get on the evening news back home. General, don't stop. We're going right past them to that van."

"But, Mr. Stryker, these are important men of your own government," protested Tobutu mildly.

"Fuck 'em! They're not the ones who have to worry about having their head setting in the cross hairs of a sniper's rifle, either. If they want to stand around out here and jerk off for the press, that's their business. We'll wait in the van."

As the distance closed between the men, the older of the two reached out his hand. Smiling he said, "General Tobutu, I'm Ambassador . . ."

The general passed the man as if he didn't exist, and walked straight to the van. Stryker shot the ambassador a disgusted look. Pushing the outstretched hand aside as he brushed by the two men, he said, "Stupid assholes."

Stunned, with his hand still outstretched to no one, the ambassador turned crimson as he realized the television crews had captured the whole thing on film. Wheeling around, he yelled, "What did you say? Now see here—do you know who I am?" screamed the embassy man as they scurried to catch up with the trio.

"Yeah," said the ambassador's aide, "just who the hell do you think you are?"

Stryker ignored both men until the general was safely inside the armor-plated embassy vehicle reinforced with bulletproof glass. Then he turned on the two men. "Yes, I know who you are—you're two fucking dicks who figured to make the evening news at the expense of my client. Is that pretty accurate, or should I repeat it louder for the benefit of the press boys over there?"

"What's your name, mister?" barked the man in his forties whom Stryker figured for a military aide to the ambassador. "We can toss your wise ass out of this fuckin' country in the next thirty minutes if we want."

Stryker's expression never changed as he tilted his head slightly and spat, "Name's Paul Stryker—and believe me, you don't want that. I go, the general goes. That's the deal. If that happens, you won't have to worry about the president seeing you boys on television—you'll be in his office. And I have a feeling that when you come out, you'll have half your ass missing. So what'll it be? A little hurt pride—or do we fly?"

"Listen, Stryker, I'm John Bach, U.S. Ambassador here. You can't do that."

Stryker spat again, "Wrong answer, Mr. Bach. We were hired to protect this man. We go, he goes. You want to make another deal—fine. But he goes with us. Come on, General, we're out of here."

Tobutu stood to step out of the van.

"No! No, that won't be necessary," said Bach. "Please stay where you are, General. This has all been a simple mistake. I suppose it would be better if we did talk at the house. We'll follow you."

Tobutu waited for Stryker's reply before returning to his seat. "That will be fine, sir. Thank you."

Bach, obviously still upset, ignored Stryker's remark and walked away. The other man remained. His cold eyes attempted to stare the ex-Green Beret down.

"And just what's your name and function around here?" asked Stryker without blinking.

"I'm Colonel Smart. I'm the ambassador's aide," said the man forcefully.

"Smart!" grinned Stryker, "Now, don't tell me. Let me guess. Maxwell, right. Maxwell Smart. That right?"

The colonel bit at his lower lip as the veins in his neck pulsated wildly. "Yes, it is! So what?"

"Oh, nothing. It just figured, that's all. We'll see you at the house, Colonel Smart, or should I say, Agent 86."

Smart's face contorted as he bellowed, "You just wait until I . . ." His words were cut short by Bach, who called from the car parked behind the van, "Smart! Come on."

Stryker smiled. "Later, 86," he said as he slid the van door closed. The arrogant grin on his face upset Smart even more.

The house provided for Tobutu was perfect for the situation. Whoever had made the selection knew their business when it came to security. It was a two-story, colonial structure, surrounded by a twenty-foot wall and a courtyard that opened out for fifty yards in all directions with the house in the center. An intruder would first have to clear the wall, then cross the open courtyard to reach the house. There was another factor that would make such a feat next to impossible. A series of floodlights hung from a series of telephone poles spaced at different intervals between the wall and the house. It would be hard for a field mouse to cross the courtyard without being observed. After adding a few touches of his own Stryker felt the general would be safe at this location. Nils and Fuller escorted the general inside while the others unloaded the luggage and their gear.

Jean Pierre came up to Stryker. Studying the layout of the courtyard, he said, "Excellent choice, don't you think?"

"Perfect," replied Stryker, watching Bach and Smart exit their car and head straight for him. From the look on the ambassador's face, it was apparent he had had time to consider the compromising position he had placed Stryker in at the airport. Smart, on the other hand, still maintained a snarl on his face and a look of pure hatred in his eyes. The ride had done little to ease the man's dislike for Stryker.

"Mr. Stryker," said Bach as he approached, "I must apologize for our earlier actions. I don't know what I could have been thinking about. Of course you were perfectly justified in your actions. Erin Richards mentioned in his communiqué that you were quite an independent individual. I see he did not exaggerate."

Reaching out his hand to Stryker, Bach said, "I hope we can put this behind us."

Stryker's icy look thawed as he took the man's hand, "Already forgotten, Ambassador."

Turning to his aide, he said, "This is Colonel . . ."

Smart rejected Stryker's hand as he growled, "We've already met, haven't we, Sergeant Major," emphasizing the difference in their ranks.

"Ex-Sergeant Major," replied Stryker, withdrawing his hand. "It's just plain old Joe Blow civilian now, Colonel. I believe we're the ones that pay your salary. So, I wouldn't want to get too nasty, Max, okay. I'd hate to have to fire you my first day on the job."

"My ass!" said Smart sarcastically.

"It'll be both our asses we fuck this up, Colonel," said Stryker. "I'll tell you what, Smart. I won't make any more jokes about your name—hell, I won't even ask if you got a phone in your shoe—and you drop the Dirty Harry routine, okay?"

"Fuck you, Stryker," was Smart's reply.

Turning to Pierre, Stryker grinned, "Oh, now look at that, Jean, only known me five minutes and already asking me to get intimate with him. Must be a Navy man."

"Gentlemen, please," cried Bach as he grabbed Smart's arm and stepped in between the two men, "we are going to be working very closely together over the next three weeks. This is hardly the way to begin. Remember, it is General Tobutu's life we are dealing with here. I suggest we cease these personal remarks and get down to business."

Stryker shrugged as he nodded in agreement. Turning to Smart, Bach said, "Now, Colonel Smart, if you do not feel you are up to this task, I have other officers I can assign to Mr. Stryker."

Smart's face dropped and he, looked like a puppy who had just been kicked by his master. "No . . . no, that will not be necessary, sir. My feeling toward this . . . this civilian's attitude is irrelevant. The general's safety shall be my major concern. Nothing else."

"Fine. Then shall we go inside? There are a number of things that we must brief the general and Mr. Stryker on before they begin the campaign."

As Bach and Smart went up the steps and into the house, Stryker and the Frenchman walked out into the center of the courtyard, where he gave orders for Pierre to get some help installing the laser-beam security system and the ground sensors they had borrowed from the CIA. He wanted them in place by nightfall. Walking back to the house, Stryker looked up and saw that Renfro and Young were already setting up their satellite communications gear. Stryker moved up the front steps feeling good. It was a feeling generated by the knowledge that he was working with professionals. He was secure in that knowledge—the knowledge that they could handle any trouble that came their way. And from the serious tone he had detected in Bach's voice, there was more than enough trouble outside those walls to go around.

Ambassador Bach's briefing was anything but brief. It lasted three hours. The ambassador covered everything from the various political factions that were at work in the country to the present status of race relations between the few white Rhodesians who had remained and the majority ruling blacks. Colonel Smart provided an assessment of Khama's military and police forces. Of key concern to Stryker was the whereabouts of Julius Keino. On this point, both men seemed less sure of their information. Keino was not an easy man to keep under surveillance. He was constantly eluding their local operatives in the city. Smart felt that since they were locals, they were fully aware of Keino's reputation. In essence, they feared the man. Julius Keino was reported to have once pulled a man's eyeball out and eaten it in front of the victim before killing him. Stryker had to admit that tailing a man like that was not exactly the most desirable job around town. He would put Charly Mangope on the streets in civilian clothes. He was familiar with the town and knew where to ask the right questions.

John Young would go along with Smart to procure the automatic weapons they expected to receive from Dibó. The ambassador had requested special authorization and exemption from Khama's policy in the case of Tobutu's private security. Bach expected the authority to be approved. At the moment, the request was in the office of the minister of internal affairs, awaiting his signature. Stryker stressed the point that he wanted the weapons, authorization, or no authorization. Bach assured him the team would have them.

Moise Tobutu was asked when and where he planned to start his campaign. He surprised everyone, including Stryker, by stating that he would begin in Harare the following morning and not in a small way, either. He planned to show up unannounced at the morning session of the parliament, where he would address a number of his former friends, as well as his enemies. Bach and Smart discouraged such a move; however, the general would not be swayed from his decision, simply stating that they had to start somewhere—they might as well start at the top.

Stryker noted the confidence in the old general's voice. If Tobutu was afraid for his life, he concealed it well. And why not? From here on out it was all or nothing.

Bidding the embassy people good night, Stryker suggested the general get some sleep. Tomorrow would begin a long three weeks. Tobutu agreed and went to his room for the night while Stryker stepped out into the warm night air of the front porch. Pierre had done his work well. The courtyard was awash in light from the poles. His eyes scanned the tops of the walls, inspecting the laser systems. Then they moved to the ground sensors. These thin rods of one-foot tubing, with their micothin wires spurting out and drooping like small fountains, would go unnoticed until a person was practically on top of them. By then body heat would have already alerted the monitoring operator of the presence of an intruder. It was a highly elaborate and effective system.

Chen Lee came out of the house and handed Stryker a message they had just received from Randy York. The backup team was in place and the choppers on station. York expressed the hope that they would not be needed. So did Paul Stryker.

CHAPTER SEVEN

Joshua Chihota walked into his office as if it were just another routine day. He was immediately greeted by a phone call from Tsonga Khama. The man was in a panic. Mosie Tobutu had just walked into the parliament building and received a standing ovation from both the house assembly and the senate.

"So what?" asked Chihota casually as he removed a cigarette from the solid gold box on his desk.

"So what?" screamed Khama. "Didn't you hear what I said? A standing ovation! We have to stop him. Have him arrested or something. His first day and already he has begun to sway those who I myself placed in high positions. This is not good, Joshua. He must be stopped."

Watching the smoke curl upward from his cigarette, Chihota could not help but smile to himself, finding humor in Khama's panic.

"Easy, Khama, there is little we can do about it now. You are overreacting to this. So he receives a little glory from old friends, so what. That will make your eulogy that much more impressive when the time comes. Should you attempt to arrest Tobutu now, you will seal not only your fate, but mine as well. Relax. Let him have his day. You shall have yours, that I promise."

There was silence on the line as Khama thought about Chihota's words, then, "Yes—yes, of course. You are right, Chihota. So what? Yes, that is fine. Let them cheer for a dead man if they wish. Thank you, Joshua. I am sorry I bothered you. I will talk with you later, goodbye."

Chihota replaced the phone. Walking to the window, he stared down on the crowded streets below. Within the hour, word of Tobutu's bold move before the parliament would be the talk of the entire city. By nightfall, the tale would have spread the length and width of the country. It was the way of things in Africa. Ignoring the long line of gray ash extending tediously from the end of his cigarette, Chihota concentrated on Khama's surprising information about the reception the old general had received from the members of the parliament. Perhaps he had misjudged Tobutu's popularity. Cheers from the poor and the gutter trash of Zimbabwe he could understand, but from the well-to-do members of the house was altogether a different matter. Most of them owed their jobs to Khama. This was a disturbing signal, but not one to become overly alarmed about. Once Tobutu was out of the way and the election over, the parliament could be replaced.

Returning to his desk, Chihota was beginning to have second thoughts about allowing Tobutu to have a free reign for a week. If he was that popular in the capital, he was sure to receive an even greater audience among the tribes of the districts. Killing a man who was overly popular could be just as damaging to them as allowing him to move about freely. It could launch an undesirable backlash against Khama's regime. "Tobutu, you old fool," said Chihota quietly to himself, "I tried to give you a little time, but now you leave me little choice. We must be rid of you before you can cause too much trouble."

Flipping through the cards on his Roladex, he found the number he was looking for. Dialing, he waited as the phone rang three times. A woman with a deep and sultry voice, answered, "Yes."

"Julius, please."

"Who is calling?"

"Tell him it's the college boy."

There was a muffled conversation before Keino came on the line. "Yes, my friend. This must be important for you to have called me here. What is it?"

The next words were like bitter pills to Chihota as he said, "You were right—we cannot afford to wait."

Chihota was forced to pull the phone away from his ear as Keino's loud laughter echoed about the room and just as quickly ended. "When?" the cold-blooded killer asked.

"Whenever you are ready. You are the professional at this, remember. You are in charge."

"Ah," laughed Keino as he said, "finally you have seen the light, my brother. We are going to work well together. Have me an office ready by the morning. I will be ready to begin my job by then." There was a pause. Chihota thought he heard what sounded like a slap on bare skin, then a woman's shriek followed by a laugh. "Don't worry about a staff, Chihota. I already have a secretary in mind, and she really knows how to take 'dick-tation' if you know what I mean?" Another laugh, then, seriously: "Don't go out tonight. Stay by your phone. You should receive a call from the police telling you of a most unfortunate incident before morning. Later."

The line went dead as Keino hung up. Chihota switched to another line and called his ranch estate located thirty miles south of the capital. Colonel Miswati, head of his private army, was called to the phone. Chihota wanted his men alerted and ready to move at a moment's notice. He would call them later with further instructions. The colonel assured him they would be ready. Replacing the phone, Chihota leaned back in his chair. If all things worked out right, by morning he and Prime Minister Khama would be rid of two problems—Tobutu and Julius Keino.

The day's events had gone well for Moise Tobutu. Not only had he received a rousing welcome home from his black brothers in the house, but from a majority of the white leaders as well. His speech, given totally without notes or prepared material, had come straight from the heart. It was a speech that told of a man's love for his country and its people. By the time it was over, even those who had at first been reluctant or suspicious of the man's motives were cheering in the aisles with the others. Even Meg Lathem dropped her macho attitude for a moment. Tears came to her eyes as she heard words she had once heard spoken by another black leader in Alabama. Words like "freedom," "equality," "brotherhood"—black and white, hand in hand, working together to restore the former greatness of the jewel of Africa. It had been an impressive speech indeed.

Overjoyed at Tobutu's acceptance in the parliament, Ambassador Bach had organized a small reception in the general's honor at the house. Guests included politicians, embassy personnel, and a few members of the press. There were the usual handshakes and backslapping going on as Stryker walked onto the porch. Moose and Nils were sitting on the steps.

"Went pretty well, today," said Nils.

"Yeah," said Stryker, his eyes scanning the walls as the last glimmers of sunlight cast a reddish orange glow against the darkening sky.

"You don't sound too happy 'bout it, boss," said Moose.

Lighting a cigarette, Stryker answered, "I'm happy for the general, Moose. I know he was worried about whether or not his own people would accept him back, but I'm afraid it's going to put us in business a little sooner than I expected."

The two men on the steps exchanged glances, then Nils said, "The old man got more support than the competition had counted on, didn't he?"

"Exactly, Nils." Studying the courtyard, Stryker asked, "Who has the first watch on the security gear tonight?"

"Meg," replied Moose.

Stryker nodded, "Okay. I know we set this thing

up for one person on every two hours, but I think we better go with two tonight. Nils, you're elected. I'll let the others know about the change." Flipping the cigarette away, Paul looked down at the Swede. "And if I see hair around your eyeballs, I'll know you fucked up again, Doc."

"Hair! Hair around your eyeballs," said Moose, "what the hell ya want hair 'round your eyeballs for, Nils? Huh?"

Stryker laughed, then turned to go back into the house, leaving Doc to explain the remark to an inquisitive Moose Sampson. Colonel Smart was standing near the door as Stryker entered. The man's attitude ranked a two on a ten scale, but he certainly could receive high marks for his choice of women. The tall blonde with the shoulder-length hair looked as if she had just stepped out of a copy of *Penthouse* magazine. Looking in Stryker's direction, she smiled a perfect smile. To say she was beautiful was an understatement. Her voice was low and sexy as she said, "You must be Mr. Stryker. Colonel Smart has told me quite a bit about you."

Stryker couldn't take his eyes off her. Dropping an arm over Smart's shoulder, Paul smiled as he said, "Oh, well, Max and I are great friends. I'm sure if you heard it from him, it was all good talk."

Her smile widened. "Well, not exactly. I'd say just enough to make you sound interesting. My name is Cheri Hogan. I'm with United Press International. I certainly wish you could have alerted us to the general's plans to speak to the parliament this morning. By the time we heard about it, it was all over."

Smart abruptly removed Stryker's arm from his

shoulder as Paul replied, "I'm terribly sorry, Ms.— or is it, Mrs.?"

"Ms. Hogan," she answered.

"Like I said, Ms. Hogan, I'm sorry. Believe me, I always make every effort to keep the press happy."

Allowing her eyes to travel the length of Stryker's tall, muscular body, she looked him in the eyes and flashed a wicked smile as she said, "I'll bet you could do that, all right."

"Mr. Stryker is married, Cheri," said Smart quickly.

That did not affect the sexy stare she was giving Stryker as she asked, "A little bit married? Or all the way married, Mr. Stryker?"

Stryker's mouth was suddenly dry as cotton. God but she was beautiful. The right answer here could mean he might have a chance to see just how beautiful she looked without the tight-fitting red dress she was wearing. "All the way, I'm afraid."

The words had just suddenly come out on their own. The reply surprised even Smart, who quickly snaked an arm around the girl's waist.

"Too bad," said Cheri, removing the toothpick and olive from her drink and rolling it teasingly along her full soft lips before darting her tongue out and plucking the olive from the stick into her mouth. Stryker was on the verge of breaking out in a cold sweat as he watched her move the olive about in her mouth. Knowing he had to force himself away from this temptress, he said, "You'll have to excuse me, I believe the general wants to see me. It was . . . nice meeting you, Ms. Hogan."

She smiled. The lucky olive still rolled about in

her moist, warm mouth. "Perhaps we can have lunch one day."

"Uh . . . yes, I'll call you." Wheeling about, Stryker walked straight across the room and directly into the bathroom. He'd have to wait for a cold shower, but some cold water on the face right now was definitely in order.

The monitoring room was lit in a dull red glow. A green haze from the scopes and computer screens was reflected on the faces of its occupants. Meg leaned back in her chair and rubbed the back of her neck.

"Tired?" asked Nils, sitting in the chair next to her.

"Yes. I wasn't when we came on duty; but now I can hardly stay awake," she replied.

"It's the equipment," said Nils. "The constant monotone of the signal from the sensors and the hum of the laser monitors will do that to you. That's why Paul limited everyone to two-hour shifts."

"So that's what it is—I wondered. This is the first time I've ever been around anything this high-tech. Thanks, Nils. For a minute there, I thought old age was catching up with me," said Meg, casting a friendly look in his direction.

"You, my dear, are a long way from having to worry about that. Look, if you want, Meg, you can go on to bed. We've only got another half-hour to go. I can handle it by myself—no problem." Quickly raising his hands, he said, "Now, I don't mean anything by that, Meg. It's just a friendly offer, that's all."

Meg was too tired to be offended or to go through her macho routine. Besides, she could tell Nils's offer was an honest one. "Are you sure, Nils?" she asked, still rubbing her neck.

"Go on—get out of here. I'll see you in the morning," said the Swede, reaching over to slap her on the leg, before stopping his hand in midair. The thought of hairy eyeballs suddenly flashed in his mind.

Meg could not help but giggle. Standing, she leaned forward and kissed him lightly on the cheek, "Thanks, Nils. Maybe I was a little hasty the other day. You're really a pretty nice guy. See you in the morning."

The scent of her perfume lingered about him as she went out the door and closed it quietly behind her.

"All right," said Nils to himself as he turned back to the control panel. "These three weeks could turn out to be a very pleasant experience after all."

Smiling to himself, he locked his hands behind his head and was just beginning to lean back in his chair when the alarm went off on the third computer screen. Something or someone had just breached the laser beam along the top of the east wall. Nils swung his chair around, and his hand went for the alert button that Young and Renfro had installed to activate an early warning system throughout the house. Before he could hit it, the number two and four screens' alarms went off. Someone was breaching the compound on three sides.

Jesus! Meg's out there, thought Nils to himself. Hitting the alarm, he pulled his 9-mm Beretta from his shoulder holster, flipped the safety off, and burst out the door just as the firing began.

Dropping to one knee, Nils saw Meg pinned down beside the front steps of the house. Ten of the intruders were already in the courtyard. Another seven were

firing from the tops of the walls. Two lay dead under
the lights, halfway to the house. Meg had nailed them
first. A line of AK-47 rounds walked their way toward
the Swede. Leaping to the left and rolling out of the
way, Nils came up firing at his aggressor, who stood
boldly atop the east wall sighting in on him again.
The man's body jerked wildly as three slugs from
the 9-mm hit him squarely in the chest, pitching him
backward off the wall.

"Nils! On your right!" screamed Meg as she released
the empty clip from her Beretta and rapidly slapped
another in its place.

Nils fell flat and swung his pistol to the right. Two
of Keino's men were coming straight at the Swede.
Muzzle flashes from the barrels of their AKs illumi-
nated their determined faces. Dirt splattered along the
side of the Swede's face, and his shirt jerked abruptly
as two bullets ripped through it, barely missing him.
Without blinking an eye, Nils squeezed off two perfect shots, each one striking its target directly in the
heart. The two men were dead before they hit the
ground.

Somewhere behind him Nils heard a barrage of
9-mm fire open up. Stryker, Lee, Pierre, and Young
had flanked Meg and were pouring it on the targets
that had made it to the middle of the courtyard. The
poor bastards never had a chance. The overhead lights
made them stand out like ducks in a shooting gallery.
Six of them went down in the hail of lead coming
from the house. Three others broke off the attack and
headed for the west wall in a vain effort to escape.
They never made it. Moose, Renfro, and Fuller were
on the roof. The three Africans ran right into their

sights and were shot to pieces; their bullet-riddled bodies crumpled against the wall. As quickly as it had started, it was over.

The courtyard echoed with the clicking sounds of magazines being released and metal against metal as fresh ones were slammed into place. Slowly the team members rose to their feet. Weapons at the ready and their eyes darting from body to body, they moved toward the dead.

"Nils, how many came over?" yelled Stryker.

The Swede signaled for him to wait a minute, then ran into the monitoring room. His eyes scanned the counters located at the bottom of each laser screen. Racing back outside, he yelled to Stryker, "Got twenty on the counters, Paul."

Stryker made a rapid count, then turned to Pierre. "I get eighteen. Right?"

"*Oui, dix-huit,*" replied Pierre. He, too, had made the same count.

A sudden rattle of gunfire broke out at the rear of the house. "The general!" yelled Stryker. "Pierre, you and Nils check these fuckers—make sure they're all dead. The rest of you split up and go around the house."

Clearing the front steps in one bound, Stryker was through the house in a matter of seconds. Reaching the back porch, he found Tobutu and Charly Mangope leaning against the wall—each with a Beretta in one hand and a can of Budweiser in the other. Two intruders, blood beginning to spread across the front of their shirts, lay dead twenty yards from the back steps. The others broke around the corners of the house. Meg and Johnny Young walked out to check the bodies. They were definitely dead. Each had four well-placed holes in his chest.

"How many?" asked Charly, holding the can of beer out to Stryker.

"Twenty," replied Stryker, taking a long drink of the cold beer and passing it back as he said, "You and the general took out the last two."

"No, no, my friend," said Tobutu, placing his hand on Charly's shoulder, "these old eyes are not what they used to be. I missed. All of my shots hit in the dirt around them. It is Mr. Mangope I have to thank for his marksmanship." Raising his beer in a toast to Charly, the general said, "Excellent shooting, Mr. Mangope."

Charly was grinning as he bumped his beer can against that of Tobutu's and jokingly said, "Well, I couldn't have done it if you hadn't kept them dancing around out there, General."

The sound of wailing sirens carried over the walls. It was Khama's police. "Ten to one they expect to find us all dead," said Meg as she walked up to the steps and placed the weapons of the two dead men on the porch.

"Nothing like betting on a sure thing, huh, Meg?" said Paul as he placed his pistol back in his shoulder holster and stepped off the porch. "Meg, get those AKs up to the Moose. He's on the roof. These cops may decide to pick up where their friends left off. Won't hurt to be ready, just in case."

Nils and Pierre were already at the gate as Stryker came around to the front of the house. The officer in charge was demanding entry. Nils and Pierre, their weapons still in their hands, refused. The officer shouted an order and his police brought their rifles up, leveling them at the two men.

"Whoa . . . here," said Stryker, stepping in front of Pierre and Nils, "no need for that, Captain. You're welcome to come on in. Too bad you didn't arrive a little earlier. You might have been able to save a few of those fellows."

"I have notified the hospital," said the African captain. "They are sending a doctor."

"I'm afraid it'll be a wasted trip, Captain. Those boys don't need a doctor, but you will need a lot of body bags."

Despite his efforts, the captain could not conceal the look of disbelief that passed over his face. "You . . . you mean, you killed all twe . . ." the man stopped himself before he said the word. "I mean . . . are you certain they are all dead?"

"Oh yes, Captain. Quite dead, I assure you."

"I . . . I see," said the officer.

Stryker was about to ask the officer if he wanted to do the report outside or in the house, when a van suddenly pulled in behind the police cars. There was a flurry of activity as Cheri Hogan and her camera crew brought out their equipment and rushed for the gate. The police quickly turned, forming a line that blocked their entry.

"Paul! Paul Stryker!" yelled Cheri. "Come on, Mr. Stryker. Remember your promise?"

Damn, thought Paul, the woman even looked great in pants, as he surveyed the tight-fitting jeans and form-fitting blouse she wore.

"Come on, Paul!" she cried. "The others will be here in a few minutes."

The captain suddenly turned on her and screamed, "Get out of here! This is not how we wish to have our country portrayed around the world. This was an isolated incident instigated by a few fanatics. That is your story! Now, go away. This is still a police investigation. Go on! Get out of here."

The woman was not only a beauty, she was stubborn as well. "Is that true, Mr. Stryker? Is the general all right?" she yelled, extending her microphone in the Green Beret's direction.

"I would advise you to agree with me, Mr. Stryker," whispered the captain. "Otherwise, I shall have to take you in for questioning. I'm sure you would prefer to stay with your friends."

"Is that a threat, Captain?" asked Stryker.

The officer's cold-eyed stare intensified as he replied, "Call it what you like. You have murdered twenty Africans tonight, American—for that alone, I can hold you for at least forty-eight hours—maybe even longer. I assure you, Mr. Stryker, you will find our jail very unpleasant. It is your choice."

"Who said there were twenty bodies in there, Captain?" asked Stryker, knowing he had the man now.

The officer knew he had screwed up. "Why . . . why, you did. I asked you, and you said there were twenty."

"Wrong answer, Captain. I didn't say shit about numbers. Now, I'll tell you how this is going to work. You get your boys to clean up my courtyard here, and we'll all call it a night. How's that?"

The veins in the officer's neck were pulsating rapidly. His eyes widened in rage as sweat began to trickle down the side of his face. Taking a step back, he pulled his pistol out and pointed it at Stryker. The men in the police line turned and leveled their guns at Nils and Pierre. Cheri Hogan and her boys went stone cold silent, shocked by the sudden turn of events. The officer's rage was now replaced by a stupid, toothy grin as he said, "So be it then, Stryker. I will arrest all of those involved in this murder. You will kindly drop your weapons and order the others to do the same. I will let my superiors decide what is to be done in this matter."

"What about the general?" asked Stryker.

"I am certain he would not become involved in such an act. He may remain here."

"All alone, huh? That should make it easy for Khama."

"I resent your accusations, Mr. Stryker. The general is no longer your problem. The murder of Zimbabwean civilians is."

The captain was becoming cockier by the minute. He figured he had the upper hand now that he had his pistol out. Cocking the hammer back on the weapon, he said, "Now, you will order your people out here, and they will come out unarmed."

"In your fucking dreams, asshole!" said Stryker in a calm tone. "What are you going to do, Captain? Kill us in front of the press? They're filming this whole thing, you know. After us, you'll have to kill all their other press friends because they'll be searching for them. Hell, Captain, you play this right, you might even manage to start a fuckin' war with the entire United States. You ready for that?"

Stryker's rapid-fire reply had the captain sweating again—that, and what he saw in the distance as he looked over Stryker's right shoulder. The cocky grin quickly faded. His eyes flashed a hint of fear. Slowly, he lowered the hammer on his pistol. He was in a bad position and knew it.

The captain's problem was suddenly solved for him by, of all people, Colonel Maxwell Smart, who had materialized from out of nowhere with a fully armed squad of U.S. Marines. Their weapons were conspicuously lowered at the captain and his policemen.

"Having a little problem, are we, Mr. Stryker?" asked Smart casually.

"You might say that, Max," answered Stryker, keeping his eyes on the captain.

Smart scanned the carnage in the courtyard as he said, "Seems you had some late arrivals for tonight's party—guess they didn't get the time right."

"Seems that way, Max," said Stryker with a short laugh. He was pleasantly surprised to find that the colonel actually did have a sense of humor equal to his own. "The captain here was just telling me that we'll have to go down to the ol' town hall to talk about this."

"The general, too?" asked Smart, pulling a cigar from his pocket and tearing the wrapper off.

"Oh no—he gets to stay here—by himself."

"I see," said Smart, lighting his cigar. "Well okay then, you all run along with the captain here. My boys from the embassy and I will just hang around and shoot the shit with the general until you get back." Placing the cigar in the corner of his mouth and his hands on his hips, Smart looked at the officer and asked, "That'd be all right, wouldn't it, Captain?"

Julius Keino was not going to be happy about this,

but what could he do? The captain had been outsmarted and outmaneuvered. They wouldn't get another chance at the general tonight. Putting his gun away, the officer ordered his men back to their vehicles. They were leaving. Smart asked about the bodies. He was told the hospital would send out the necessary people to remove them. Shouting at his driver to move out, the captain and his police sped away into the night.

Cheri Hogan ran up to the gate. Directing her photo people to get lots of pictures of the courtyard, she turned to the two men. "You're both crazy, you know that, don't you? You were within a hairsbreadth of provoking a shoot-out in which both of you would have certainly been killed."

"Not really, darlin'," said Stryker as he lit a cigarette.

"How can you say that, Stryker? I stood right over there and watched the entire thing."

"The eyes, Ms. Hogan. The man knew if he shot me, he was a dead man. He'd take one right between the eyes."

"But, you didn't even have your gun out," she protested.

"Didn't need it." Paul smiled. Reaching out, he took her by the shoulders and moved her to the exact spot where the captain had been standing. "Now, stand right there." Looking back over his shoulder, Stryker yelled, "Hey, Joe! Mind giving me another sight picture?"

Turning back to Cheri, he said, "Now, look over my shoulder and tell me what you see."

The girl moved her head slightly and saw a man

with a rifle on the roof of the house. The weapon was pointed at them. "I see a man on the roof with a rifle pointed at you," she answered.

Stryker laughed. "No, honey—not me. It's sighted in on those pretty eyes of yours. That's a fellow we call Moose, he can knock a coffee cup out of your hand at five hundred yards with an AK-47. I have a feeling the captain knew that. Fortunately, Colonel Smart arrived before Moose had an opportunity to show off his talents. Thanks, Colonel."

Smart had moved in close to Cheri after seeing a glimmer of admiration in her eyes for Stryker's sort of insane courage. "No problem, Stryker. The general phoned the embassy immediately after he heard the sirens. We got here as quickly as we could. Any of your people hurt?" he asked.

"Naw, just the bad guys. When are we supposed to get those guns from Dibó?" asked Stryker.

"In three or four days," replied Smart.

"I'd like to see if we can't speed that up, Colonel. The Beretta is a great little automatic, but it's no match for AKs."

"That can be arranged," said Smart.

"Good." Turning to Cheri, Stryker said, "Ms. Hogan, I believe you'll find the general on the front steps. I'm sure he wouldn't mind expressing his opinions to an attractive lady of the press. I'll have my boys keep the others out until you're finished. Kind of an exclusive, you know."

"Thanks, Paul," she purred.

"That's me. 'Old bend-over-backwards-to-help-the-press Stryker,' they call me," laughed Paul.

Winking as she brushed past him, she whispered,

"Now, that's a position I've never tried."

Stryker felt the hot flashes returning. "You got any cold water on you, Colonel?" he asked.

"What?"

"Never mind. Come on inside. I'll show you how this thing went down. I'm sure Ambassador Bach is already on the phone to Washington. The brass will want to know all the details."

"You can count on it," said Smart, flipping his cigar out into the street and following Paul Stryker across the bloody battleground of the courtyard. It was going to be a long three weeks.

CHAPTER EIGHT

Captain Dekunta stood in silence before Julius Keino and Joshua Chihota. Both men were upset and highly irritated with the failure of the raid on Tobutu's residence, as well as Dekunta's inability to remove the security people from the site in order for Keino to undertake a second attempt. Fearing to say any more than necessary, the captain now wished he could return the money Chihota had paid his men and him and simply walk away from this situation. However, Dekunta was a realist, and as such knew that that option no longer existed. He and the eleven other policemen he had bribed to join him were now in this thing until the end. Keino would personally kill anyone who attempted to back out now.

"You say this man—the American they called Stryker—was the one in charge. Is that correct, Captain?"

"Yes, sir. And a very cool customer he is, sir. If he

was worried that I would kill him, I never saw it in his eyes, nor in his face."

"Then you should have shot him," grunted Keino. "Then you would have seen a change of expression, I am sure."

"As I stated, Mr. Keino, one of his men was positioned on the roof with a rifle pointed directly at my head. Had I shot the man, I would not be standing here now. For that matter, I doubt any of my men would be either. These people are highly trained professionals, Mr. Keino. You have only to take a trip to the morgue and observe the pattern of bullet holes in the bodies of your men to see that I am correct."

Keino frowned at the captain as he barked, "You and your men should have entered into the fight with the others. If you had, we would not have this problem."

Now it was Dekunta that was becoming irritated. The entire mess at the house had been Keino's idea, not his; and he would tell him so. "That was not the plan, Keino—you said . . ."

Keino sprung from his chair with remarkable speed. Before Dekunta could react, Keino's hand shot out, slapping the captain hard across the face. "You insolent bastard! Don't you dare attempt to hide your cowardice by suggesting it was my plan that went wrong."

Chihota raised his hands. "Gentlemen, please! What is done, is done. Arguing the point is a waste of time and is now immaterial to the problem. Mr. Keino, please return to your seat. Captain Dekunta, are you all right?"

The side of the captain's face felt as if it were on fire. It had been a vicious openhanded blow. For a second, Dekunta considered going for the pistol on his hip. The only thing stopping him was Keino's personal bodyguard, the big man they called Sebota. The giant held an Uzi machine gun in his hands and was watching the captain's every move. If his hand moved toward the holster, Sebota would cut him in half with the automatic weapon.

Keino suddenly laughed as he said, "Ah, I just saw something in your eyes, Captain. It is too bad this Stryker did not slap you. Perhaps then you would have done your job."

Ignoring Keino's continued baiting of the captain, Chihota attempted to get back to the problem at hand. "Captain Dekunta, can you find out what locations Tobutu is planning to visit tomorrow?"

With the pain in his face gradually easing, the captain averted his eyes from Keino's mocking stare and replied, "Yes, I believe I can, sir. I still have a contact within the American Embassy, but it will be expensive. My sister-in-law will not risk her job with the Americans cheaply."

"No matter the cost, Captain," said Chihota, "we must have that information, and we must have it before noon tomorrow. Get this information, Captain, and I will throw in a bonus for you as well."

"Hell," snorted Keino, "the bastard has already been rewarded—I haven't killed him, yet."

"Please, Mr. Keino, I will handle this, if you don't mind," snapped Chihota. "Now, Captain Dekunta, can you accomplish this?"

Still avoiding Keino's eyes, he answered, "Yes, sir. You shall have your information before noon. Is that all, sir?"

"Yes, Captain. Thank you."

Dekunta nodded. Wheeling about, he moved swiftly to the door of the old warehouse, all the time feeling the eyes of Sebota on his back. The captain did not begin breathing normally until he had stepped out into the warm night air.

"We should have killed the little bastard," swore Keino as he watched the door close behind Dekunta. "If it had not been for our need for the information, that is exactly what I would have done."

"Do not worry about Dekunta, Keino," said Chihota, sliding his chair back and rising to his feet. "If this American Stryker and his people are as efficient as the captain has said, then, he and his fellow policemen will not be with us this time tomorrow night."

Keino's laughter filled the abandoned warehouse as he, too, stood. "So you intend to use his men for the attempt tomorrow?"

"Naturally. They are the police. They can get closer to Tobutu than your people could ever hope to. Then it shall fall to you to hunt down the assassins. Once they are eliminated, we will be free of witnesses, and you will become a hero."

"That sounds good, Chihota; but, unless I am mistaken, there will be no one left for me to eliminate, and the plan will fail," said Keino in a matter-of-fact tone.

"Would you care to enlighten me as to why?" asked Chihota.

Turning to the man, Keino made a fist, then, extended one finger in the air. "First, the man was right about one thing—this Stryker and his people are professionals." Another finger went up. "Second, I sent twenty of my best men up against them and all twenty died. Counting himself, Dekunta has only twelve. Third, the idiot forgot to recover the weapons my twenty men were carrying when they were killed. Therefore, the American now has not only the fifteen-shot Berettas but also automatic weapons as well. If they could take out twenty of my people with handguns, just imagine what they can do with an AK-47. No, my brother—if I were you, I would want more than a one-day schedule from his sister-in-law, because, like you said, by tomorrow night, I have a feeling Captain Dekunta will no longer be with us."

"My God! Even I forgot about the rifles," cried Chihota, surprised that he could have missed something that important. To have been reminded by a man he considered a mutant from the Stone Age only made it worse.

"I can rectify that error in the morning. I will call Ambassador Bach and tell him the weapons used in the attack are essential for our investigation."

Keino shook his head. "No, Chihota, I would rather wait. Who knows? Dekunta and his men may get lucky. If they don't, then we are rid of him—courtesy of this man, Stryker. Should that happen, then you can confiscate the weapons as my men and I organize another attempt."

Chihota was amazed. There were times when this man appeared perfectly sane and completely rational—hell, even brilliant. Too bad it only came in short phases between the killing and mayhem. "Very well, then, that is what we will do."

"We!" said Keino sarcastically, bursting into laughter. Wrapping his arm around Chihota, he began moving toward the door. "Sorry, Chihota, but for a moment I had a vision of you with a gun in your hand and facing down this man Stryker."

Chihota responded with a halfhearted laugh of his own as he asked, "And did I back him down?"

Keino laughed again, "No, brother—you were pissing in your pants!"

At that moment, Joshua Chihota experienced the ultimate in humiliation as Keino's fellow Neanderthal and bodyguard, Sebota, gave out a chilling laugh that was a cross between a sick burro and the joyous cry of two hyenas at the height of intercourse.

The mess in the courtyard had been cleared away and dirt tossed over the pools of blood, erasing any signs of the violence that had taken place less than ten hours before. Smart and his Marines had remained at the compound until daylight, just in case Stryker had any more unexpected guests. At breakfast, Stryker made a futile attempt to convince the general to postpone his appearances—at least until they had a positive fix on Julius Keino. The general flatly refused. Messages which were sent to WISCO and CIA Director Hayes requesting assistance with the problem came back negative. They would continue to check their sources.

During the night, Colonel Smart, Stryker, and Charly Mangope discussed the possibility of sending Charly out onto the streets in civilian clothes to see if he could pick up a lead on the terrorist and a possible location of his headquarters. Smart had agreed. For intelligence purposes it would be a good move; however, it could prove extremely risky for Mangope. The man would be out there all alone. No one from the embassy or the team would be around to help him if he ran into trouble. That point didn't seem to bother the Shona warrior and former Rhodesian noncom. Charly had walked out the gates just before dawn this morning and already Stryker found himself wishing he had vetoed the idea. He had a bad feeling about it.

The general went upstairs to get dressed for the trip to the town of Gatooma, the first stop of five scheduled for the day. Stryker had a bad feeling about that too, but the general was as stubborn as he was gutsy. Pulling a cigarette from the pack in his shirt pocket, Stryker walked out onto the front steps and lit it. Johnny Young came bounding out the door and past Stryker. "See you later, boss," he said.

"Where you going, Johnny?" asked Stryker.

Young stopped and, looking rather surprised, replied, "With Colonel Smart, Paul—you know, to pick up the weapons from Dibó."

Jesus, thought Stryker, *I'm losing it.*

"Hell, that's right, Johnny. Sorry 'bout that—must be time to pay for all those brain cells I killed off drinking that Jack Daniel's over the last twenty-five years. Go ahead, and be careful."

"You got it," said Young as he went to the gate to wait for Smart to pick him up.

Meg came outside and joined Stryker on the steps. Opening the morning paper, she pushed toward him as she said, "That little gal that keeps giving you a hard-on don't cut much slack in her writing, does she?"

"Damn, Meg, you really got a hell of a mouth on you, you know that?" said Stryker, taking the paper from her hands. "You know, you don't have to play this macho hard-ass crap all the time. We all like you. You don't have to try to impress anybody."

"Really, Paul," she answered in a sincere little-girl voice that Stryker had not heard before. "You know, I always wanted to have a lot of friends when I was growing up. Wanted to be liked by everyone. Popular—ya know. Have good-looking guys ask me out and bring me flowers and all that stuff. I wanted them to like me—treat me like a lady, ya know. Not cuss me or slap me around like my old man did my mama. But, it just never worked out that way." Patting her large breasts she continued, "I had these big knockers, even when I was a kid. Pissed all the other girls off 'cause their boyfriends would start droolin' at the mouth every time I walked by. They started callin' me a slut and a whore—all kinds of other vile shit, and there I hadn't done a thing to them. The guys I did go out with only wanted to get their hands on the tits or in my pants. I wouldn't let 'em so they started callin' me a tease and tellin' their friends they'd laid me, and that I wasn't nothin' but a tramp. Hell, Paul, I didn't even lose my cherry till I went in the army. Even the damn drill sergeant had to get me drunk to get that. Guess all those years of pain and hurt just kinda built up inside me so long I had to let it out. The army was just the place for that. They respected me in the army. I mean, they at least gave me a chance to prove how well I could do things, and each time I did they rewarded me with a damn medal or a pat on the back, but at least it was something positive. The men respected me—women still envied my tits, but we were sisters in army green, so that made us friends. Guess that's why I always played the hard-ass. I didn't want to lose my friends. That make any sense, Paul? Or am I just rambling on like some dizzy broad with a bad case of PMS?"

Stryker leaned over and kissed away the tear that had begun making its way down her cheek. "Perfect sense, Meg. Thanks."

"For what?" she said, wiping the water from her eyes.

"For sharing that story with me. I got a feeling you don't tell it to many people."

"Not for a long, long time, Paul," she said, standing and brushing the dust from the seat of her pants. "That lady friend of yours sure can write. Thought you might want to have a look at that. I'm going in for some breakfast. Are we still out of here at 0900 hours?"

"That's it, kiddo," said Stryker, "and thanks for the paper."

Turning his attention to the paper, he saw the picture Cheri's cameraman had shot of the killings in the courtyard. The man had used a wide angle lens in order to get the maximum number of bodies in the photo. The press loved the shock value of such pictures—it sold a lot of papers. Meg was right. It was a hell of a story. It was a good bet that Prime Minister Khama was already on the phone to the sexy lady's editor. Although she never accused Khama of direct involvement in the night attack, her story contained plenty of highly speculative remarks that could only point in Khama's direction. Not only was the lady intelligent and beautiful; she had balls as well. Max was a lucky man.

Although the officer and gentleman had not said a

word, Stryker knew that the lucky bastard was playing bumper cars under the sheets with the lady. He could see it in the way Smart looked at the woman as she moved into a room. He hovered around her when other men came near her—like a wolf that marks his territory, then prowls the perimeter to keep others out. Smart was lucky, all right, but Stryker couldn't shake the feeling that the relationship was a one-way deal on the colonel's part—not Cheri Hogan's. She was far too much of a flirt. The woman radiated pure sex, and her suggestive little remarks were hardly those one expected of a woman in love with only one man. Just as he was fooling himself by thinking that he could take this woman for a wild ride around the bedroom without feeling guilty about Sharon, perhaps Smart was fooling himself in his belief that Cheri really cared about only him.

"Oh, screw this," said Stryker, folding up the paper and standing up.

"And just what is it we are going to screw, Paul?" asked Tobutu, standing in the doorway.

Momentarily embarrassed that the general had overheard the remark, Stryker replied, "Myself, if I don't get my shit together. I take it you're ready to go, sir." The general nodded that he was ready.

Jesse Fuller and Moose were just rounding the corner of the house. Stryker yelled for them to bring the vehicles around. Going into the kitchen, he told those at the table to bring their chow with them if they were still hungry. It was time to move out. Calling to Pierre, who was at the top of the stairs, he told him to get everyone outside and not to forget the AK-47s.

*　　*　　*

Captain Dekunta struggled to control the queasiness in his stomach as he leaned against a wall across from the main plaza. The crowds had begun to gather hours before in anticipation of Tobutu's arrival. Banners and signs adorned practically every building in the small town of Dueiti. That was to be expected. This was Tobutu's hometown, and the last stop of the day for the local hero.

Dekunta didn't like this. He didn't like it at all. Chihota and Keino had tricked him. They had lured his men and him into this evil plot and were now threatening to expose them all unless they did this dirty work for them. Keino was the murderer—the terrorist expert—he and his cutthroats should be the ones doing this, not Dekunta and his men. If only he had been as smart as Chihota and recorded their conversations. However, hindsight was of little value now. Chihota had them. He had only to say that he was working undercover to expose the plot and he could walk away free. No, Dekunta and his men had no choice now. They had accepted their fate. The only way out was to kill Tobutu and get it over with.

Glancing nervously at his watch, he saw it was half past four in the afternoon. The general was scheduled to arrive at five. Each second that ticked away seemed like hours to the captain. He and his men were dressed in civilian clothing, not the police uniforms Chihota had preferred. That was insane. No, if Dekunta was to pull the trigger, it would be done his way. He had two marksman on a rooftop two blocks away. They were the finest sharpshooters he had, and today they would have to be. The distance where Tobutu was expected to make his speech was over seven hundred yards from the roof to the podium. To have placed them any closer would not have been wise. This man Stryker was no fool. Dekunta knew that upon their arrival, Stryker would place his own men atop the roofs in the immediate area of the plaza before allowing the general to step up to the podium.

As insurance, he had five of his men dispersed in the crowd to the right of the stage; three more were on the left, and he and two other men were directly across from the stage area. If the sharpshooters missed, the task would fall to them. Either way, Tobutu would be killed today. Once the deed was done, they would fade away in the confusion and panic of the crowd. Their only worry was Stryker and his team. The stage was set. Now, all they need do was await the arrival of the victim.

The general's spirits were high. There had been nothing but massive crowds showing support at every stop throughout the day. For Stryker and his people, each stop, each speech, had been an exercise in nervous tension at its highest level. The fact that, with Young and Mangope gone, they had only eight people to keep an eye on everything and everybody only added to that tension. The team was glad that Dueiti was their last stop.

As the caravan of vehicles reached the outskirts of the small town, people lined the sides of the road cheering as the general drove by. Tobutu shook his head sadly as he noted that nothing had changed in all these years. His people still lived in poverty. Where were the improvements that had been promised? The planned housing and government buildings were nowhere to be seen. Tobutu didn't have to ask. He knew where—in the pockets or bank accounts of Khama and his asshole friends who were living in luxury while the people lived amid the squalor and filth that had existed for them all too many years.

As the cars approached the edge of the town, the crowds grew larger and the cheering louder. Stryker reminded the general to remain in the car until he came for him. The few constables of the town attempted to clear a path for them to the stage. Reluctantly, the people moved aside until finally the cars stopped in the plaza. The security team stepped out, seriously perusing the area. Their weapons were clearly visible. People, frightened, moved back, clearing a path for the armed men. Having only eight people, Stryker directed Pierre and Moose to the rooftops of the two tallest buildings around the square. He wanted Fuller on the stage with him. Nils and Meg would remain on the ground in front of the podium. Lee and Renfro were to be at the rear of the crowd and to the left and right.

Waiting until he had received radio confirmation in his earpiece that all personnel were in place, Stryker then moved to the car and opened the door for the general. The crowd broke into a screaming, howling chant of, "Moise! Moise! Moise!"

Tobutu waved to the people as he made his way up the steps of the improvised stage to the podium. Fuller moved to the right corner of the stage and immediately began to scan the crowd. Stryker did the same from the right. Whispering into the small mike on his collar, he told Moose and Pierre to stay on their toes. The show had begun.

Dekunta smiled to himself. The American had done exactly what he figured he would do by placing two men on the roof. His two sharpshooters were a block over and behind Stryker's men. Easing their rifles over the edge of the rooftop, they sighted on their target. Flipping the safeties off their weapons, the men began to take up the slack in the triggers, totally unaware that Dekunta, for all his planning, had overlooked one important detail. He had placed his snipers facing east.

Moose Sampson and Pierre saw the flash of sunlight off the scopes at the same time. There was no time for precision firing, and they both knew it. Moose yelled a warning to Stryker over his radio mike, while at the same moment cutting loose with a burst of AK-47 fire that stitched its way along the brick-and-tar-paper edge of the roof. Pierre did the same. The snipers ducked for cover as the bullets tore a deadly path only inches above their heads. On the ground, Stryker covered the distance to the general in one flying leap and threw him to the floor of the stage. Fuller, his Beretta in his hand, quickly spotted two of Dekunta's men moving in from the left. They were using the panic-stricken crowd as shields to allow them to get closer to the stage. Fuller knew he could take them out, but not without hitting the civilians in the process. "Nils! Meg! Coming at you on the left!" he yelled, as he dropped to one knee, holding the sight of the 9-mm directly on the head of one of the approaching men. Nils and Meg, moving in a crouch, waved their pistols and tried to motion the people to get down so they could spot the targets. At the same moment, Dekunta waved for his men on the right to close in for the kill. More rifle fire echoed into the plaza from the rooftops. People were screaming and scrambling for cover as gunfire erupted all around the square.

Stryker pulled another Beretta from inside his belt at the small of his back and pressed it into the general's hand. Pieces of wood were splintering all around him and Tobutu as the five men coming from the right opened up on the stage. "General, when I open up, I want you to round off the backside of this stage and stay there. Anybody but my people stick their heads around there, you blow it off, you hear. Now, get ready, here we go."

Stryker leaped to his feet and fired three quick shots just over the heads of the fleeing civilians, hitting two of the attackers squarely in the chest and slamming them backward. The angle of his position on the stage gave him an advantage on the other three, but there were still too many innocent people running between them.

Meg saw her target first. The man held an elderly woman in front of him and was pushing her toward the stage. Meg couldn't deliver a killing shot without hitting the woman. Seeing Fuller positioned for a clear shot, she yelled, "Jesse! I'm going to kneecap him! Be ready."

Fuller nodded and took up the slack in the trigger of the Beretta. Bringing her gun up in both hands, Meg timed the man's shuffling motion forward, breathed deeply, released half the air, and squeezed off the shot. The round hit the man in the kneecap. He screamed and spun halfway around. At the instant the man turned, Fuller placed two shots cleanly through the side of his head.

Nils saw the second attacker push his human shield to the side for a shot at Meg. That was all the room he needed. Extending his arm, he squeezed off two shots. One hit the man in the chin; the other blew away the right side of his face.

On the rooftop, the rifle battle was still going on. Pierre crawled to one corner of the roof at a left angle to the snipers. Signaling Moose to fire a burst, he waited until the big man finished firing, then he counted, "One thousand, two thousand, now!" Rising suddenly, he caught a man with his head exposed concentrating on his fire at Moose. Pierre's rifle was on single fire. One shot was all he needed. The bullet struck the unsuspecting sniper just above the right ear, exploding the man's head like a watermelon. In panic, his partner jumped to his feet and ran for the back of the roof. Moose rose, sighted the AK ten yards behind the fleeing man and squeezed off a burst of automatic fire that sent a trail of bullets biting into the tar paper and walking a straight line right up the middle of the man's back. The impact of the rounds sent the man airborne and over the side of the building.

Meg, Nils, and Fuller all sighted in on the final man on the left and fired at the same time, tearing him to pieces. Lee and Renfro were moving in on the three men on the left when Stryker yelled, "Lee! Look out, behind you!"

The warning came too late. Dekunta and the two men at the wall with him had gone to the ground among the civilians. They had waited to see how the battle went before committing themselves. Lee and Renfro were standing with their backs to Dekunta. It was too tempting to ignore. Coming up on their knees, the three men were about to fire when Stryker yelled. Lee reacted by leaping into the air, performing an oriental roll and diving to his left when he hit the ground. All four shots fired at him had missed their target. Renfro was not as fortunate. Twirling about, he managed to get off one shot which barely missed Dekunta before a flurry of six rounds ripped through his body, killing him before he hit the ground.

Seeing Stryker on the stage reloading his weapon and Meg and the others far to the right, he decided it was a good time to try rushing the stage. Yelling for the three remaining men on the far left to advance, he ordered the two with him to move forward. Once again, Dekunta made two fatal mistakes. One was the amount of time it takes a professional to reload a Beretta—especially in the heat of battle; and two was that he forgot about the people on the roof. That mistake, however, was quickly realized as the stunned man saw all three men on his left torn apart like rag dolls by a hail of AK-47 fire from Pierre and Sampson. The two he had ordered forward froze for an instant before turning to run back to the wall. Stryker put three rounds in one man's back. Blood shot out of the man's mouth as he tried to scream. It splattered the front of Dekunta's shirt. The second man was hit in the arm, but managed to make it back to the captain's side. Together, they ducked into a building a few steps away.

Stryker jumped from the stage, shouting that he wanted at least one of them taken alive and that the others were to surround the exits. He went after them.

Pausing in the doorway, Stryker bobbed his head in the doorway, then quickly pulled it back again. Two shots chipped the brick where his face had been only a second before.

Meg started to edge her way to the other side of the doorway. Stryker shook his head no; he wanted her to stay outside. Kneeling, he counted silently to himself before he dove through the doorway into the darkened room and rolled to the left. A string of wild shots came from two sides of the room. Moving silently along the wall, Stryker's hand came in contact with a tin can. Picking the can up, he readied the pistol. He tossed the can toward the darkened wall near the door. Three shots rang out. Stryker, seeing the muzzle flashes, emptied his entire magazine in that direction. There was a loud groan and the sound of a table crumpling under the weight of the body that had fallen on top of it.

Reloading again, Stryker heard another sound. A man was moving on the wooden steps that led to the second floor. Moving quietly, his eyes adjusted to the darkness. He stopped at the base of the steps and listened. Nothing. Easing his weight onto the first step, he slowly made his way upward. Still hearing nothing, he moved to the fifth step, then, to the sixth. Maybe the man was already on the roof. Pressing his weight down on the seventh step, he started to move, when suddenly the step gave way and his boot crashed through the rotten wood, throwing him off balance and backward. His gun slammed into the railing and fell away into the darkness below. "Shit!" he said in disgust.

"My feelings, exactly, Mr. Stryker," said Dekunta

from the top of the stairs. His gun pointed down at Stryker in his compromising position. "That was exactly how I felt watching you slaughter my men out there a few moments ago." Moving down the steps slowly, Stryker could make out the white of the captain's teeth as he smiled. He had Stryker and he knew it.

"Somehow, this is going to make it all worth it, Mr. Stryker. You know, it is a small compensation perhaps for what I have lost; but, still, I shall enjoy it very much."

Stryker waited for the flash that he knew was about to come from the barrel of Dekunta's gun. "You going to talk me to fucking death, or what, Captain?"

"Arrogant to the end, aren't you, Stryker. Very well, I would prefer to do this slowly, a piece at a time. Would you care to beg for your life before I end it for you?" asked Dekunta jokingly.

"The lad only begs for pussy and Jack Daniel's, ol' boy," said a voice from behind Dekunta. The startled captain turned. In the two seconds he was alive, he saw only the outline of a man at the top of the stairs; then, there were four rapid flashes and a burning sensation as the four slugs ripped through his body, slamming him backward rolling him end over end down the stairs. Dekunta was dead by the time he rolled over Stryker.

The sudden flashes had totally wrecked Stryker's night vision, but he could hear the man at the top of the stairs making his way down to him. Then, "Sure and be damned if I didn't warn you them big feet of yours were going to be gettin' you in trouble one day, laddy. Now, look at ya all stretched out there like a whore on her day off. It's a bleedin' shame. I can tell that."

Still lying on the steps with his foot hung up, Stryker pulled out a cigarette and lit it as he said, "How you been, Willy? Didn't think you were coming until later in the week. What happened? They throw your Scottish ass out of Panama for wearing your kilt?"

Willy McMillian chuckled as he replied, "Naw, laddy—that wasn't the problem. Just the opposite, as a matter of fact. I couldn't keep any clothes on. Too many damn pretty women down there you know. Some of 'em even married. Guess it was the kilt that drove 'em crazy. Wanted to know what was under there, so I just had to show 'em, you know what I mean?"

"Yeah," said Stryker, turning his head as he heard someone enter the room. Willy shifted his gun toward the door. "It's okay, Willy, they're my people."

"Yeah, I know. I was watchin' the ruckus from a second-story window across the street. Afraid I was moving over this way when one of your boys went down. Sorry I couldn't help him. You okay?"

Stryker took a last drag on the cigarette and tossed it away. "Just a little cramp in my leg, but other than that, I think I'll make it. You want to help me out this fuckin' hole?"

Willy laughed, "Jesus, laddy, I done killed a fellow for you, now you want me to do manual labor, too. You bloomin' Yanks never change," he said as he bent down and pulled Stryker up, working his foot out of the broken step.

From below, Meg called out, "Paul! Are you all right?"

"I'm fine, Meg. How's the general?"

"Not a scratch, but he's mad as hell. All the hit team were cops. Khama's cops."

"Yeah, I know. The same ones that were at the house last night. What about Renfro?"

"He didn't make it, Paul," said Pierre, "and I'm afraid three civilians were killed as well. Not by us— by the bad guys. Guess that doesn't matter much when you're the one that's been killed, does it?"

Stryker limped down the stairs and made his way outside into the fading light of the day. The general was talking to his people, who had gathered around the cars. Nils, Moose, and Lee were keeping them a respectable distance from the old man, not wanting to lose him after all this. "Willy, thanks for savin' my ass. I owe you one. I'll introduce you to everyone when we get back to the safe house. Right now, I think we better get out of here. I don't want to be on the roads after dark any longer than we have to. Pierre, get 'em loaded up. Put Renfro's body in my Land Rover. I'll take him to the embassy when we get in and make the arrangements to send him home. Let's move it. Willy, you ride with me. I'll fill you in on what we know up to now, which isn't much. Charly Mangope should be able to fill in some of the missing pieces when we get back. Till then, all I can tell you is they take their damn elections fucking serious over here."

"Ah, yes, ballots and bullets—politicians and corruption, democracy at its finest," said Willy. "As long as they maintain those ingredients, I'll always have a pot to piss in and women to chase. It's a grand thing— democracy—yes, indeed."

*   *   *

Ambassador Bach was waiting for Stryker at the embassy gates when he arrived with the body of Mike Renfro. Tsonga Khama was outraged. Three innocent civilians had been killed, and it had been reported that the deaths were the direct results of automatic weapons fire from Tobutu's security force. That was a clear violation of Khama's standing order on the possession and use of such weapons. Bach was to confiscate the weapons at once and turn over those responsible for the killings of the civilians. Reports of the violations and the incident had already been wired to Washington by the Zimbabwe government.

Watching the Marine guards remove the body bag and place it gently on a stretcher for the trip to the morgue, Stryker turned to Bach and said, "Screw that bastard! It was his own damn police that attempted the assassination."

The statement did not have the shock value Stryker had thought it would. "We know," said Bach, uncomfortable about having to discuss this over the body of a dead American and member of Stryker's team, "Khama has already released a statement that Captain Dekunta and his men acted solely on their own. A press conference was called at the ministry. Joshua Chihota, the internal affairs minister, showed a hidden video recording of a meeting between Dekunta and an undercover agent. Dekunta openly admitted that he and his men were going to assassinate Tobutu. Even Chihota was in on the sting operation. They say that before they could act on the evidence, Dekunta changed the plan and hit you at Dueiti."

Stryker stopped at the doors to the morgue. "All

pretty clean-cut and neatly wrapped, wouldn't you say, Ambassador?"

Bach watched through the window as the bloody body of Mike Renfro was removed from the bag and placed on a table. Turning quickly away from the sickening sight, he replied, "Yes, Paul, I know, but it's a perfect wrap job. The evidence cannot be disputed. It's all on video. How is the general taking all this?" asked Bach.

"He's doing fine, sir. He's back at the house and secure. This is about what he expected all along. Just started a little sooner than we figured." Stryker paused and thought for a moment, then asked, "I suppose you have a file on this Joshua Chihota. Could I have a look at that before I leave?"

"Of course. Come on upstairs and I'll get it for you. You think he's involved in this?"

"Could be. I'm just a little curious as to why a minister would suddenly want to play James Bond knowing he was walking into a nest of assassins. The man's either got balls like an elephant or he was involved a lot deeper than anyone knows," said Stryker.

Reading the folder on Chihota took an hour. By the time he was finished, Stryker had made a few notes on a pad. He then provided Bach with the information that would be needed to ship Renfro's body back home. WISCO would pick up the tab. Walking to the door, Bach called to him, "Paul, I . . . I'm afraid I'm going to have to insist that you turn over those AK-47s today. I'll send some of my people by to pick them up in an hour. They'll turn them over to Chihota. Sorry, but Khama was especially insistent on that point. They have to be turned in by tonight."

Stryker nodded, "I'm sure he was. I'll have them ready for you in an hour. I won't need them anymore, anyway. Colonel Smart and Young should be picking up our weapons from Dibó along the South African border right about now. If Khama wants those weapons, he'll have to come and get 'em himself—and that won't be easy, I promise you that. Goodbye, Ambassador."

Keino placed his hand on the arm of the man with the sniper rifle. "Wait, not yet. Let them get all the weapons transferred and the South Africans leave. We want only the Americans."

The sniper nodded and continued to watch the action below through his scope as Dibó's men removed cases of ammo from their truck and placed it in Colonel Smart's Land Rover. Keino slid back from the lip of the ridge, motioning for his men to take their position to the left and right of the road that passed through the small pass which led back to Harare. The Americans would have to pass this location to return to the capital.

Satisfied that his men were well hidden, Keino returned to the ridge. Bringing his binoculars up, he studied the group of men below. He recognized Dibó, the French gun runner from South Africa. He had ten of his own men with him. The tall American opening the briefcase that contained the money for the deal was Colonel Maxwell Smart of the U.S. Embassy. Keino didn't recognize the others, but figured at least one or two of them had to be Stryker's men. The others were also American, Marines from the embassy more than likely. Altogether there were eight Americans. That should prove no problem for Keino. He had fifty men with him.

Dibó and Smart shook hands and the two groups departed in different directions. Keino moved swiftly down the hill and signaled his men that they were coming. Taking cover himself, the terrorist leader released the safety on his AK-47 and waited for the fun to begin.

The embassy Rovers made their way up the twisting, bumpy road, which was filled with ruts caused by the summer rains. Young and Smart sat beside the driver of the lead vehicle. They had not yet heard of the attack at Dueiti. The lead Rover rounded the small hill of the main road. The driver looked down to shift into low gear. The sniper's first round shattered the windshield, striking the young Marine directly through the top of the head. Blood seemed to explode within the confines of the cab, splattering both Young and Smart. "Jesus Christ!" screamed the colonel, as the Rover veered wildly to the right, ran halfway up the hill, and flipped over. The dead Marine fell on top of them, pinning them in the cab. Three more bullets slammed into the vehicle as the other two came under fire. Two Marines from the second Rover leaped out and were immediately gunned down by the horde of Africans lining the small ridge on both sides of them.

Johnny Young managed to wedge himself free. Crawling out of the cab, he reached in and pulled Smart out of the smoking Rover. Smart was covered in blood from a deep cut along his forehead. Half-dazed, he looked up and muttered, "Look . . . look . . . out!"

Young released the man's collar; at the same time he pulled his Beretta from its shoulder holster and whirled about. He came face to face with three charging Africans wielding long-blade machetes. Young snapped off four rapid shots that downed two of the attackers, but the third was on him before he could shift his fire. The razor-sharp blade of the long knife came down with a heavy thud as it sliced Young nearly in half. Placing his foot on Young's chest, the native pulled the blade free and raised it to deliver a blow to Smart, who had passed out cold. Seeing the amount of blood around the American officer's head, he decided not to waste the time. He ran over to join in the butchering of the remaining Marines.

Signaling for his vehicles to be brought up, Keino ordered the weapons and ammo loaded before they departed for the capital. The sun hung low in the east. It would be dark soon, and he wanted to be back in Harare before midnight. He was anxious for news of Dekunta's success or failure.

Dibó gently wiped the blood from Smart's face as the colonel slowly began to come around. "Wha ... What, happened? Where ... where are ..."

"Easy, my friend. The others are dead. You are fortunate not to be among them," said Dibó wringing out the cloth and pouring more water on it before placing it on Smart's head.

Smart tossed the rag aside and struggled to his feet as he asked, "The weapons?"

"Gone, my friend. They took everything."

"But how?" asked Smart. "How did they know the time and place? I just don't understand it," said the colonel, moving a few feet in the last glimmers of the afternoon sun. "They had to . . ." Smart stopped suddenly. Kneeling down beside a body lying on the side of the hill, he felt his stomach wrench. It was Charly Mangope. The sides of his chest had been sliced open and the shimmering white objects that reflected in the setting sun were his ribs. Someone had reached inside the man's chest and broke them outward. Moving back from the horrid sight, Smart saw something near his boot. Bending down, he started to reach for it, recoiled, turned, and vomited. It was one of Mangope's eyeballs. It had been bitten in half.

CHAPTER NINE

The mood around the Tobutu safe house was one of solemn silence. News of the death of Mangope and the embassy Marines, coupled with the loss of Renfro on the same afternoon was too much even for these hardened soldiers of fortune. It was as if the entire operation was coming loose at the seams. The general was seriously thinking of pulling out of the race and returning to America. If this many people had already died before the elections, how many more would join the dead afterwards? Even Rutherford and Richards were beginning to have their doubts about the feasibility of continuing the struggle. The team had been shaken by the rapid sequence of events, but kept their opinions to themselves. They had been paid to do a job. They would remain until it was completed or until WISCO pulled them out. Depressed by the turn of events, yet more determined than ever, Stryker spent the remainder of the night checking the perimeter and talking with the team members on duty. Stryker had fully expected another attack on the compound that night, but as morning broke all was quiet.

The general had canceled his trips for the next few days. After speaking with his sons by phone he had settled into an even deeper state of depression. The information from the Chihota file that Stryker wrote down was transmitted to WISCO. Stryker knew that if anyone could confirm his suspicions about Joshua Chihota, it was Erin Richards and the vast intelligence network of WISCO. Stryker would have answers to his questions by nightfall.

McMillian, seeing Stryker across the courtyard checking the vehicles, went over to his old friend. Dropping his foot up on the bumper of one of the Land Rovers, he asked, "Heard any word on Colonel Smart's condition?"

Stryker went through the motions of checking the oil as he answered, "Slight concussion, cuts and abrasions, and a bullet hole through his right leg that he didn't even know he had. All in all, they say he'll be okay. Dibó got him to a hospital in South Africa. Bach and I figured it best to leave him there."

"Listen, Paul, I want you to know, if I'd known this thing was going to be this tough, I would have gotten here a lot sooner."

"I know that, Willy, thanks. The thing is, you're here now, that's all that matters. I have a feeling it's going to get a lot worse before it gets better. We're restricted by Khama's rules, while all he has to do is keep sending people at us night after night. I'm afraid it's just a matter of time before he wears us down. Hell, we may even pull out in the next few days. It really depends on Tobutu. He may figure it's already cost us too much. We'll just have to wait and see," said Stryker as he jammed the oil stick back into place in frustration.

True to his word, the ambassador's men had come for the weapons last night. Once again, the team would have to rely on only their 9-mm pistols to protect the general. Stryker suggested that the ambassador issue them weapons from the embassy. Although fully understanding Stryker's situation, he could not allow that. The M-16s could easily be traced back to the embassy and provide Khama with even more propaganda to use against the United States in his claims that America was interfering with free elections in Zimbabwe.

"You know, Willy, just once I'd like to fight a fuckin' war without political bullshit calling the shots. Can you imagine that? I mean not having to kiss anybody's ass to get permission to launch an attack or chase the bad guys across a border and kicking their asses without the threat of a court-martial hanging over your head when you got back."

Willy shifted the chew of tobacco in his mouth and spit as he laughed and said, "Yeah, Paul, and I also dream about having a twelve-inch dick and laying five different women in a day. I'll make you a deal, you give me my dream, and I'll see about workin' on yours for you. What do ya say?"

Stryker laughed for the first time since this had all happened. "Twelve-inch dick, my ass. Hell, then you couldn't wear that cute little minikilt of yours in public without your peter showing. Come on, I'll buy you a cup of coffee."

As the two men entered the house, Stryker saw Tobutu on the phone. He overheard him say, "Yes, Chihota. Of course. I shall be there within the hour. Thank you."

Grabbing Willy's arm, Stryker said, "Wait a minute, Willy. Let's see what's going on here." Crossing the room, Paul asked, "Excuse me, General, but was that Minister Chihota on the phone?"

The old man was smiling again as he replied, "Yes, Paul. Good news. Chihota is willing to sign the special weapons authorization and provide us with an escort wherever we wish to go from here on out."

Tobutu saw the looks of suspicion exchanged between the two men. "Do not worry, Paul. This was not Chihota's idea. It was demanded by a special session of the house and passed without a single no vote. Even Khama is not foolish enough to go against the entire house. The escort is to be selected by a party of both white and black members of the legislative parliament committee to assure reliability. I trust them, Paul. I saw their eyes the other day when I spoke. The same desires I have, they have. It was in their faces. I cannot win an election by hiding myself away in this house. I must go to the people. Now, would you have a car brought around. I must go to the ministry office. Khama wishes to show his support for the parliament's decision and has called a press conference. I would not want to be late."

Further argument was useless. The general was going, with or without Stryker and his people. Stryker rounded up the team while Willy brought the car around. The convoy formed, they headed for the ministry office. Arriving, Stryker saw Cheri's news van among the number of press vehicles. Maybe, just maybe, all the killing had put so much heat on Khama that he was going to back off and let the chips fall where they may in a free election. Stryker wanted to believe that. But then, Willy wanted a twelve-inch dick, too.

The conference room was crowded with members of the parliament, press people, and embassy personnel. If anyone was going to hit them, they figured it would have happened before reaching the conference. Tobutu was applauded as he entered the room. Stryker glanced at Willy and shrugged his shoulders. "Maybe we were wrong."

Willy shifted his pistol within easy reach as his eyes roamed about the room and the railing around the second floor of the room. He whispered, "Maybe, but I don't feel my dick growing any, ol' boy."

"Come on, Willy, you can't believe they'd gun him down in front of all these people," said Stryker.

"Yeah, well, tell that to Lee Harvey Oswald next time you see him."

Seeing Stryker near the doors, Cheri passed her microphone to one of the crew as she walked up to him. "Mr. Stryker, how are you? I'm glad to see you permitted the general to attend. Hopefully, this will put an end to all the needless bloodshed."

Stryker was about to answer her when Willy shoved them both to the floor and pulled his Beretta at the same instant. One of Keino's men opened up on the crowd from the second floor railing with one of the 9-mm Mini-Uzis stolen from Smart.

Meg and Pierre leaped on top of Tobutu, hauling him to the floor. Meg's body jerked as three rounds ripped through her back. The lone gunman was joined by three others. Willy nailed one of them before having to dive for cover behind a nearby table. Stryker raised his head in time to see Chihota pushing Khama through a side door and closing it behind them. When others tried the same exit, it was locked. Those seeking entry were gunned down where they stood.

Scrambling across the basketball-court-sized room, Nils got off a flurry of shots that sent another of the men toppling to the floor below. The sound of gunfire was deafening in the confines of the room. Sliding in next to Pierre, Nils saw the bloodstains spreading across the back of Meg's shirt. He went insane. Leaping to his feet, he took down another of the men on the second floor as he made a dash for the stairway. Shoving Meg's gun into the general's hand, Pierre joined the Swede at the foot of the stairs. "You ready?" yelled Nils, dropping his empty magazine and loading a fresh one.

"*Oui, mon ami*, for Meg," answered the Frenchman, jumping ahead of Nils and taking the stairs three at a time. Two of Keino's men turned and pointed their weapons at Pierre. They hesitated too long. Pierre pumped four shots into the first one and two into the second one, with Nils adding three more for good measure. Racing along the corridor, the two men took on another two men that were coming out of one of the rooms with weapons in their hands.

Willy kicked the double doors behind him open, and rolled out into the hallway. A line of 5.56 slugs from a Beretta AR-70 assault rifle sent a fountain of sparks off the marble floor less than six inches from him. Before the terrorist could fire again, Stryker dove, slid across the slick floor on his back, and fired two shots that took the man's head off. Grabbing Willy by the pants leg, he dragged him out of the line of fire and behind a fountain. "Makes us even, ol' boy," he said, reloading.

Suddenly it was quiet again. The firing had stopped. Heavy clouds of gunsmoke hung over the hall like a London fog. Stryker's first thought was of the general and Meg. Dashing back into the conference room, he saw Nils and Pierre covering the main room from the balcony. Willy ran in behind Stryker. Lowering his gun, he whispered, "Oh, shit."

Tobutu was gone. Only Meg's bullet-riddled body lay near the overturned table that had contained the documents the general had come to sign. Dropping to his knees, Stryker set his gun aside. Rolling Meg Lathern over, he cradled her head in his lap. Tears were in his eyes as he slowly wiped away the blood that had trickled down the side of her mouth. She had saved Tobutu's life with her own. Holding her tightly, Stryker pulled her still body up and rested her head against his shoulder. He wept silently for the little girl who had only wanted people to like her.

A note had been left by the those who had abducted the general. They claimed to be a group known as the Rhodesian Freedom League, former Rhodesians who had fled to South Africa at the time of the peace settlement. A radical group, they were said to be led by former white Rhodesian officers who made their headquarters in South Africa. Neither Stryker nor Willy believed a word of it. When Tsonga Khama publicly went on the airways with a blistering speech that blamed all the attacks on Tobutu's life on South

African influence, both men knew they were right. Khama needed a scapegoat, and the league was elected. Practically all of the press people bought the story. All but Cheri Hogan, who not only appeared to have doubts, but seemed to know that the story was a fabrication of total shit.

With the death of Meg, Stryker had become a man obsessed. Ambassador Bach attempted to calm him as they stood in the communications room of the embassy awaiting official word from Washington as to what policy was to be pursued in light of the new situation. Stryker insisted that policy was no longer an issue in the matter. If Khama could convince enough people that South Africans had perpetrated the attacks against Tobutu, he could use that hatred to enrage the people into a war with South Africa, thereby having an excuse to postpone the elections until a settlement of the matter was agreed upon.

It all made sense to Stryker now. Whoever had orchestrated this mess was a true virtuoso of American policy and the political game. Within the hour, the Washington reply was coming over the secure teletype equipment at the embassy. Stryker read each word as it appeared.

TO: Ambassador Bach,
    U.S. Embassy, Zimbabwe
FM: U.S. Department of State.
    Believe situation has deteriorated beyond acceptable purposes with the abduction of General Tobutu. High ranking staff and advisors believe it highly unlikely that general will survive more than twenty-four hours, if not dead already.

You will reestablish solid relations with present government and offer all necessary assistance to assure Prime Minister Khama that we are fully behind him 100%. Inform WISCO personnel that their services are no longer required and see that they are out of the country within next twenty-four hours. END OF MESSAGE.
.... NOTHING FOLLOWS ... .

Stryker cursed under his breath as he read the communiqué.

"Sorry, Paul," said Bach with sincerity.

Stryker tore the copy of the message off the machine and crumpled it in his hand. "For what? This! This don't mean shit, Bach. You hear me —not shit!" Stryker was beyond the point of being mad. He was killing mad.

"Now, wait a minute, Stryker. Those are direct orders from the State Department. You have to obey them just like I do."

McMillian stood in the corner, trying to get Bach's attention. This was not the time to pull rank on Stryker. One of the Marines at the teletype, worried about the tone in Stryker's voice, and feeling that his boss needed some backup, started to stand up. Willy placed a hand on the boy's shoulder and pinched the nerve in his neck, as he whispered, "Now, you don't get in the middle of this, laddy—you ain't got enough rank, me boy. So you just sit quiet, okay?"

"You're all the same, Bach, you know that? You start the shit in the goddamn world; then, after people have been slaughtered and killed because of your screwed-up policies, you simply change the fucking rules and go like nothing happened. Well, not this time, buddy. This time we're going all the way. No more fucking rules; no more bowing down and getting set up by these assholes. They've killed four of my people and abducted the general. You think I'm going to just walk out there and go home like those people never existed? Well fuck you, too. They want a fucking war—by God, I'll give them a fucking war— only this time on my terms. You or anybody else try to interfere and you'll be history before the damn sun sets. That's not a threat, Bach—it's a fucking promise. Come on, Willy, let's go get the general back before these assholes let Keino kill him for convenience."

Bach was still yelling about the consequences of such actions as Stryker and Willy walked out of the embassy.

Chihota sat in the shadows of the warehouse as he watched Keino beating Tobutu. The blows were slow and dealt with a viciousness that showed only the pleasure the abuser received from his work. For Chihota it was both sickening and strangely exciting. His problem was solved, or at least half the problem. There was still the matter of ridding himself of Keino. His earlier plan for executing the man was no longer feasible. The situation had changed twice already. No, there had to be another way. He would not know peace until both Tobutu and Keino were eliminated. Then it came to him. Of course. With the present situation, even Keino would be suspicious. He would have the terrorist take Tobutu to his ranch to the south. There Keino could play his sadistic games as long as he wanted. After the general was dead, they could cremate him and scatter the old fool's ashes over his beloved Zimbabwe. It sounded good to Chihota. Naturally, Chihota would have Colonel Miswati and the Rhodesian rifles waiting for them; then they could cremate the whole damn lot at the same time. With their problems solved, things should go back to normal. He arose to call to Keino, but hesitated. He wanted to watch a little longer.

"Moose, you sure you know how to use this thing?" asked Pierre as he watched Sampson hook up the black box to the satellite on the roof of the safe house to receive a set of photos Stryker had requested from Richards.

"Sure, Frenchy, ain't nothing to it. Used to help Johnny Young with it all the time. Sure miss that little peckerhead," sighed the big man, switching on the receiving elements and computing the angle of the miniature disk. Looking at his watch, he said, "Okay, Pierre, when I say, I want you to switch on that Nicad-Battery pack. One, two, three, now."

A low hum came from the assortment of boxes and equipment Moose had interconnected to the disk. As if by magic, the fax signal receiver-printer came to life, and one by one a series of photos began to roll their way out of the machine. In less than two minutes, the satellite contact was over. Moose shut down the equipment while Pierre took the six photos they had received downstairs to Stryker.

The living room of the house had been turned into a wartime operations center. Maps and photos covered the west wall. Nils, Lee, and Willy were stripping and cleaning the automatic weapons they had recovered from the dead men at the ministry building. As Pierre entered with the photos he had just received, Stryker was on the phone with Randy York in South Africa. A secure scrambler attached to the phone line assured that their conversation, even if monitored by Khama's secret police, could not be understood without a matching scrambler.

Seeing Pierre, Stryker said, "Just a minute, Randy. We just received the sat photos and information I requested from Erin."

Cradling the phone between his cheek and shoulder, Stryker read the cover letter and went through the photos.

"Randy, it's just as I thought. Chihota has three different bank accounts under various names—two in Europe and one in Central America. Judging from these amounts, the man's been ripping this country off for a long time. Looks like he's got his own army, too. Sat photos of a ranch he has about thirty miles from here show maybe fifty, sixty men in fatigues and armed to the teeth. It's a good bet that if Tobutu is still alive, that's where we'll find him. That will be our primary target."

Stryker noted the apprehension in Randy's voice as the former major replied, "Damn, Paul, have you thought what is going to happen if we're wrong on this? I mean this guy is the internal affairs minister of that country. We go storming in there like Rambo, blow the place all to hell, and there's no General Tobutu—well, I don't have to tell you the rest of the story, do I? All I'm saying, Paul, is we have to be sure

Tobutu is there, otherwise, we could find ourselves facing the entire armed forces of Zimbabwe."

Stryker knew York was right. Chihota was as crooked as a snake and had so far managed to amass a fortune while covering his ass on all sides. If Stryker was wrong about the ranch and Tobutu, there was going to be hell to pay—at least for anybody still alive after it was over. "I know, Randy," said Stryker, and a hint of uncertainty was noticeable even in his own voice. "I wish I could tell you that I had positive confirmation that the general was there, but I'm afraid I can't do that."

"Yes, you can, Stryker, Keino's got him," said a familiar voice from across the room. Stryker turned to see Maxwell Smart hobbling into the room. A cane supported his weight and a bandage surrounded his head. "Tobutu will be at Chihota's ranch by first light tomorrow," said Smart with confidence.

Stryker told York to hold on while Willy helped the colonel to a chair next to the phone. "Are you positive of that, Max? How reliable is your source?" asked Stryker.

"One hundred percent reliable," answered Smart. "Got it straight from Sidney—I believe Tolbridge told you about his top agent here, right?"

Stryker nodded, then relayed the information to York. Moving to the map on the wall, Stryker gave Randy the coordinates for the location of Chihota's ranch. It was just approaching dusk. Stryker and his team would move out for the ranch at midnight. They would take up positions around the ranch and wait for the arrival of Keino. Quickly calculating the distance from York's location along the South African border to the ranch, Stryker figured it would take the backup team two hours flying to reach the area. York agreed with the calculations. He would have the choppers and the team in the air by 0400 hours. That should put them at Chihota's at exactly dawn.

"Okay, then, Randy, guess that's it. No need to tell you that if you don't make the show, our asses are out. With those gunships and backup, we're outnumbered eight to one. Just don't stop for coffee and doughnuts, okay?" said Stryker with a laugh.

"You got it, sport," replied York. "See you in the morning. Good luck, Paul. Out."

Disconnecting the scrambler, Stryker told Willy to gather up what was left of the team and bring them to the room. While waiting, Stryker asked the colonel how he was doing. His leg was still stiff, but his headaches had stopped. He was still a little beat-up, but he wanted to be in on this thing. "Do you know how many men Keino has with him?" asked Stryker.

Smart grinned as he said, "Not nearly as many as he had before you folks got here. You've been cutting his numbers down pretty quickly over the last few days. Even Sidney's not sure of the count, but fifteen to twenty would be a good ballpark figure."

Stryker didn't expect an answer, but asked the question anyway, "Max, just who is this Sidney character?"

Max shook his head. "Hell, Paul, you know I can't tell you that. Tolbridge would have my ass."

Stryker shrugged his shoulders. "Yeah, I figured I'd just ask."

Counting Stryker, there were only seven members of the original team left. Not what one would call a mighty force, but their combined experience more than made up for the shortage of numbers. Stryker went over the information he had and the plan of attack. The key was York and the choppers. Without them, they wouldn't have a chance, and they all knew that, but that vital fact was never once mentioned by anyone in the room. This was what they did for a living, and they did it well. Stryker completed the briefing by asking if there were any questions. There were none. They all knew what they were going to do, and why. Nothing else needed to be said. They would leave at midnight.

Across town, Ambassador Bach prepared a drink and handed it to Sidney. "Do you think they can actually pull this off? I mean, my Lord, they're only seven men and a crippled colonel against Chihota and Keino's forces."

Stirring the drink slowly, Sidney replied, "If anyone can do it, it's Stryker and his men. I was against Smart going along at first, but after he told me what he saw at the ambush, I could better understand his reasons for going. Has Stryker contacted Mr. York, yet?"

"Yes, about a half an hour ago, according to an agent there. They are to be airborne by 0400 hours, arriving at Chihota's at first light."

Sidney nodded in approval while sipping at the drink. "Excellent. Good man, that Dibó—a little sloppy on that weapons exchange business, however, still a good man. The choppers and backup team should even up the odds a little, I would think."

Placing the drink on the table, Sidney stood and said, "Well, I'd better get going. I don't want to miss the show."

Bach was stunned, "Why, surely you're not planning on going to Chihota's ranch?"

"Of course. I wouldn't miss it for anything. Besides, Stryker might need an extra gun before it's over. Just make sure that you have Khama and the press at the ranch by eight o'clock. The battle should be over by then; and no matter which way it goes, we have to put the prime minister in a situation where he cannot deny Chihota's involvement in this entire affair. Therefore, it is imperative that he and the press are there before the smoke clears."

Bach assured Sidney that he would have them all there at the proper time, and bid the CIA agent farewell. Returning to the bar he poured himself a stiff drink and seriously contemplated another line of work. This business was not helping his ulcer in the least.

Stryker and Lee moved silently through the darkness until they reached the chain-link fence that surrounded the Chihota ranch. It was two in the morning, and most of Chihota's army were asleep. Four men with rifles sat along the front of the well-lit porch. Another three were patrolling the perimeter of the fence. Lee pointed out another two standing in the shadows near the motor pool. Fifty yards to the left of the house were two long, barracks-type buildings. These were the long houses provided as quarters for the main forces. If Stryker's estimates were correct, they contained over fifty men. Moving quietly back from the wire, he and Lee rejoined the others. Stryker passed his observations on.

He broke them down into two-men teams. Pierre and Nils would work their way around to the left rear of the long houses and take up positions there. Lee and Fuller would move to just behind the motor pool and hold there. Stryker, Willy, and Moose would settle in near the main gate. Smart, because of his condition and mobility problems, would remain outside the fence and use the Navy Arms, SKS 7.62 39-mm rifle with a scope that Dibó had given him. He would take out targets of opportunity once the action started. Checking their watches and testing the small collar mikes attached to their pocket radios, the men moved out for their assigned positions to await daylight and the arrival of Keino and Tobutu.

Stryker's team remained quietly in position for three hours when Pierre came up on his radio to report a bustle of activity going on inside the troop billets. All the lights were on; the commanders were shouting orders and running the men out of the buildings. Stryker parted the grass and watched the reported activity, wondering what was going on as the men hastily fell into formation with their weapons slung over their shoulders.

A big barrel-chested man moved to the front of the group and began issuing more orders. Stryker especially missed not having Mangope with him now. Now no one on the team spoke the language; therefore they had no idea what the man was telling his troops. Looking at his watch, the commander turned toward the horizon, then back to the men before shouting another command. The formation broke ranks and scurried off in every direction around the compound, taking up concealed positions behind buildings, Land Rovers, and trees. Only a small group remained in the open with the big man who walked to the gate, slowly making his way toward the house. He stopped every now and then and directed his soldiers to hide themselves better, or move to another position. Stryker glanced over at Willy as he whispered, "You thinking the same thing I am?"

Willy, smiling, whispered back, "Double-cross."

Stryker nodded. "You got it. Chihota's going to take out Tobutu and Keino at the same time." Whispering into his mike, Stryker passed the information on to the others. This was an unexpected surprise and would work to their advantage. Stryker ordered his men to hold their fire until the shoot-out began between the two forces. They would make their move once the action started, using the confusion to their advantage. Everyone was to watch for any sign of Tobutu and make every effort to secure the man before he was killed. Other than that, there were no friendlies inside the wire.

Stryker glanced over his shoulder at the horizon. The ashen gray of the predawn had begun to rise like a magic curtain. It was 0545. It would be light in fifteen minutes. Willy tapped him on the arm and nodded toward the winding road that led to the ranch. Four vehicles, their headlights still on, were making their way up the road. It was Keino. Chihota sat beside him. The minister had not planned to come along, but Keino had insisted and Sebota had enforced the order by literally picking him up and tossing him into the Land Rover. Attempts to conceal his nervousness were strengthened only by the belief that once they were in the compound, he could signal Colonel Miswati to abort the planned slaughter of Keino and his men. It was his only chance, and he knew it. One shot and Keino would kill him. The guard at the main gate stepped out. Recognizing Chihota, he opened the gates. Colonel Miswati and five of his men were standing in front of the house, waiting for them.

Tobutu, half-beaten to death, lay unconscious in the back of the second vehicle. Keino saw the surprised, confused look on Miswati's face as he recognized Chihota sitting beside him.

"Get ready," said Stryker into his mike. "It's going down."

Chihota could see the befuddled look in his commander's eyes. This was not going to work. It was obvious to Chihota that the men had already been deployed. Normally, there were twenty or thirty of them milling around at this time of the morning. The Rover stopped directly in front of the colonel. Chihota was sitting nearest to the door. Opening it, he stepped out and suddenly flung it back in Keino's face, knocking the man back across the seat. "Kill them!" screamed Chihota, making a mad dash for the house and safety.

Miswati and his men brought their pistols up and blew the driver away as he attempted to exit the vehicle. Keino dove into the back seat and out the back drop window. Crawling to the corner of the Rover, he leaned around and emptied a seven-shot clip of .45-caliber rounds into the two men standing next to Miswati. The entire compound suddenly erupted in a storm of ear-shattering gunfire.

"Tobutu has to be in one of those vehicles," yelled Stryker. "Go! Go! Go!" The team broke from cover and into the compound, taking on targets from all directions. Willy cut loose on the two men at the gate, taking them down with two short bursts and kicking the gates open. Smart, lying prone outside the fence, dropped two of Chihota's men before shifting his fire to one of Keino's boys who was racing for the fence and what he thought was safety. Lee and Fuller blasted the three men hiding in the motor pool. Afterward, they scrambled over the fence and behind a pile of lumber for cover. Pierre and Nils caught four soldiers rounding the barracks in the open and opened fire. The four went down in a hail of lead.

Zigzagging across the open ground with bullets hitting all around him, Stryker was throwing lead from the Beretta at anything that moved as he neared the second vehicle. Less than ten yards away, he felt a stinging sensation along his right leg. He stumbled. Falling, he hit the ground and rolled up against the front tires of the Rover. A Keino man stepped around the rear of the Rover. Leveling his weapon at Stryker, he suddenly recoiled. A chunk of his head flew off. "Nice shot, Max," whispered Stryker, pulling himself up by the door handle and looking inside. The general was just coming to. His face was a bloody pulp and his hands were tied. Moving to the back door, Stryker jerked it open and leaped inside just as the side windows of the Rover were shot out. "Get down, General," he yelled, crawling over the seat and into the back storage area. Placing his pistol down, Stryker was untying the general's hands when a soldier darting by, stopped, and peered inside through the rear glass. Tobutu grabbed Stryker's pistol and shot the man in the face. His hands free, Tobutu kicked open the tailgate and slid down behind the Rover. Stryker was beside him. Grabbing the dead man's AK, he yelled, "Come on, General. Head for the house."

Dirt flew up behind the two men as they made the relative safety of the front porch. Across the way, Lee and Fuller were driven out from behind the stack of lumber by intense rifle fire from one of the barracks. They were caught in the open. A cloud of dust rose up around their feet. It seemed every rifle in the place had zeroed in on them. Fuller was hit in the chest. The round spun him around and three more hit him in the back, slamming him to the ground. Lee jerked as a bullet tore through his left leg and sent him spinning like a sand crab into the dirt. Another round struck him in the shoulder, knocking him forward. Through the force of sheer willpower, the tough ex-Red Chinese officer ignored the pain and pulled himself to cover behind an overturned barrel. Moose scrambled to Lee's side and laid down a barrage of automatic fire that drove a squad of oncoming soldiers back to cover.

All about the ranch the gun battle continued as small groups of men converged on each other in the deadly game. Keino, his cheek sliced wide open from a bullet fired by Nils, dove through an open window into the house. He was looking for Chihota. He had seen the coward run inside when the battle started. Moving from room to room, Keino suddenly stopped. He heard the sound above the roar of the gunfire outside. It was the sound of helicopters. Moving to the window, he looked up in time to see two gunships level out and make a gun run that wiped out the few men he had left in one pass. The giant, Sebota, stood up. His dirty white shirt was covered with small red dots. The big man wavered for a moment before falling like a giant redwood, face-first into the dirt.

The back door slammed. Keino whirled and ran through the house. Through the window, he saw Chihota running for the barn. "You bastard!" he swore, looking down to place a new magazine in his .45. "Now, I'll get your ass." Jerking the door open, Keino came face to face with Paul Stryker.

"Going someplace, motherfucker!" said Stryker with a smile as he fired two rounds point-blank into Keino's stomach. The man doubled over and fell backward; his gun fell from his hand. Looking up, he screamed, "Go on, you bastard! Finish it."

Stryker stepped through the door. "This is for Charly," he said, firing a shot from the side that tore Keino's left eye out. "This one's for Meg." The Beretta exploded again; this time its target was the left kneecap. Keino screamed. "And this one is for all the innocent people you've butchered." The third and final shot hit the man in the center of the forehead. Smoke was still exiting the hole as Stryker turned away. He went out the door to search for Chihota.

The gunfire had slackened to only a few scattered bursts here and there as York and the backup team searched out those that had survived the gun runs by the helicopters. Walking across the yard, Stryker saw Tobutu heading for the barn. He yelled to him, but the general continued on. Running to catch up, Stryker reached the doors of the barn just as a series of shots rang out.

Stepping inside, his pistol leveled for action, Stryker saw Tobutu standing over Chihota's body, which lay slumped against the bumper of a Rolls Royce. "You okay, General?" asked Stryker, lowering his gun and walking up to stand next to Tobutu.

"Yes, my friend," said the general, his mouth bleeding from broken teeth and one eye swollen shut. "I've never felt better."

Willy was at the doors, "Hey chaps, we got visitors coming. Looks like the ambassador and the whole friggin' army of Zimbabwe. Oh, yeah, and your news boys, too."

Stryker and Tobutu walked out into the morning sunlight to greet their visitors. Prime Minister Khama, revolted by the general's appearance, immediately began to offer his deepest apologies. He had no idea Joshua Chihota had been involved with the murderer, Keino. He was thankful that Tobutu was still alive. The people would be elated at the news. The cameramen and photographers were having a field day filming the death and gore that lay all around them.

Joining Randy York at the choppers, Stryker watched as Lee was placed aboard. Nils had loaded him up with morphine. Lee was smiling like the cat that ate the canary, oblivious to the pain from his two bullet wounds. Next came the body bag containing the body of Jesse Fuller. There would be no more airport security jobs for the ex-Marine. This trip, he was the VIP.

"Sorry we were late, Paul," said York. "Hit some bad winds that slowed us up."

Stryker slapped York on the back and grinned, "Hell, partner, you got here, that's what counts. Any of the backup team hurt?" he asked.

"No one dead. Got a few boys shot up a little, but nothing serious."

Smart was brought to the chopper on a stretcher. Stryker looked down at him and asked, "The leg bothering you, Max?"

Smart shook his head sadly as he replied, "You believe it! The bastards shot me in same goddamn leg again."

Stryker laughed. York waved for the teams to start loading up, then, turned to Stryker, "The ambassador tell you our job's finished here?"

"No, I haven't talked to him yet. He's over there getting all the publicity he can with Tobutu. So, who's going to watch over the old man when we're gone?"

"The U.N.; Khama wanted to make sure he wasn't linked to Chihota, so he called the United Nations in to monitor the elections and assure the safety of the candidates. After watching the war you were having over here, they could hardly say no. They'll be here tonight. Then, we go home."

"Home! Now there's a word that has a great sound to it," said Stryker, "And you, Randy York, you come to visit anytime, but if it's business, don't waste the time. I'm permanently retired after this one."

"Yeah, right," grinned York. "Like that James Bond movie says, 'Never say never.'"

Stryker said his goodbyes to the ambassador. Tobutu, who refused a handshake, instead hugged Stryker as if he were one of his own sons. Waving so long, he slid onto the steel plating of the chopper as it prepared to lift off. Smart was lying next to the door. Stryker leaned over and yelled, "Hey, by the way—thanks for the head shot you did on that joker that had me cold beside that Land Rover."

Smart shook his head and yelled back, "Wasn't me! I was reloading. It was Sidney."

"No shit!" said Stryker. As the chopper began to lift, Stryker saw Cheri Hogan in all her gorgeous beauty waving to him. He hadn't seen her arrive with the others. Leaning back over Smart, he yelled, "You know I never did ask Cheri where she was from? Do you know?"

"Sure, mate," yelled Smart with a grin. "Australia—Sydney, Australia."

They survived Armageddon
to sail the oceans
of a ravaged nightmare world

OMEGA SUB   76049-5/$2.95 US/$3.50 Can
On top secret maneuvers beneath the polar ice cap, the
awesome nuclear submarine U.S.S. *Liberator* surfaces to
find the Earth in flames. Civilization is no more—great
cities have been reduced to smoky piles of radioactive ash.

OMEGA SUB #2: COMMAND DECISION
                76206-4/$2.95 US/$3.50 Can

OMEGA SUB #3: CITY OF FEAR
                76050-9/$2.95 US/$3.50 Can

OMEGA SUB #4: BLOOD TIDE
                76321-4/$3.50 US/$4.25 Can

OMEGA SUB #5: DEATH DIVE
                76492-X/$3.50 US/$4.25 Can

OMEGA SUB #6: RAVEN RISING
                76493-8/$3.50 US/$4.25 Can